Stone of the Sea

Stone of the Sea
A novella

Jeanette O'Hagan

Story 3 Under the Mountain series

By the Light Books

Stone of the Sea: a novella
By Jeanette O'Hagan
Story 3 in the Under the Mountain series

Cover design: Jeanette O'Hagan © 2018 ,2019
Typesetting and Layout: Jeanette O'Hagan
Copyright Jeanette O'Hagan © 2018, 2019 http://jeanetteohagan.com

NLA Cataloguing-in-Publication entry at National Library of Australia:

 A catalogue record for this
book is available from the
National Library of Australia

ISBN-13: 978-0-6481640-5-0

Published through By the Light Books
By the Light Books PO Box 2520, Brookside Centre, Qld 4053
Email: Bythelightbooks@gmail.com

Note: This book follows Australian style conventions for spelling, punctuation and grammar.

Subscribe to Jeanette O'Hagan's Newsletter for the latest on new releases, giveaways and other news– http://eepurl.com/bbLJKT

Dedicated to my brother, Tom,
with whom I've shared many an adventure.

Delvina squinted against the molten glare of the sun rising above the Cauldron's sheer cliffs. Golden light mixed with blue-grey shadows splintered across the forested floor and transmuted the surface of the crescent lake into silver fire. Dazzling splotches of light and shadow danced across her vision. The strange sharp smell of pine and sun-warmed rock and wide outside spaces tickled her nostrils.

She shaded her eyes. 'Where?'

'There.' Thirdwun Danel moved closer and pointed to the left of the blazing furnace in the sky.

A dark silhouette spiralled down into the Cauldron from the east, the early light glinting on its feathered wings. Delvina suppressed a shiver as the great beast seemed to swell in size and detail, the white gleam of the fangs in its long snout catching the sun's rays. Unlike the bats or small birds that inhabited the outer caves, the koraktil had four sturdy limbs with curved claws, a powerful chest, and a long sinuous tail. Its wings stretched more than three paces long. Not that it would hurt them, for it was one of the Adelphi returning with supplies from the Great Forest. Zadeki's father, Korak, by the size and markings.

'About time,' Secondwun Nebam growled as he strode towards them with a bluster his mother, the new Overseer and leader of the realm, avoided. 'Surely these abovegrounders know the sun burns our skin.'

'That's why they're ferrying in supplies now,' Danel muttered from behind them.

The Secondwun showed no sign of hearing the comment and Delvina swallowed words in the Forest Folk's defence. They'd been at these five nights already, and everyone's nerves were frayed with lack of sleep and half rations. Working outside without the comfort of solid rock above their heads only added to the tension. The Outside was terrifying, and she could understand Retza's hesitation about braving it again. Yet, since their return to the tunnels she had felt constricted and closed in. She wanted to see more of the world.

The koraktil dropped below the tops of the pine trees and angled toward them, his tail snaked behind him.

'Can't see the others,' Secondwun Nebam muttered, pale eyebrows scrunched over his narrow face.

The skies above the tall cliffs remained empty of the other two koraktil. Only the faded half-circle of the smaller of the two moons and a few wispy clouds broke the blue.

A flurry of pine needles and the sudden rush of wind flattened her fringe against her face. Korak's shadow blanked out the sun, bringing blessed relief to Delvina's burning skin. Flight feathers spread and wings fanning, he landed in newly cleared space in front of them.

She rushed forward and clambered on the rock beside the shapeshifter. Hands still chilled from her early morning vigil in the open air despite the growing heat of the sun, she fumbled at the straps of the harness strung across Korak's back. With a grunt, she pulled the knots free, and unfastened the first of the panniers. Expecting a heavier load, she took a step back and lost her balance. She would have tumbled off the rock had Danel not caught her.

'Steady there.'

'Be careful, Prentice,' Nebam barked. 'By the pit, we can't afford to spill a single scrap of food.'

Delvina bit down on a sharp reply and lowered the woven container to Danel who passed it to the Secondwun. She and Danel moved to Korak's other side. Once again, she passed down a half-empty container, before jumping down from the rock.

Nebam dug his hand into the edible roots, fruit, and mushrooms. 'Is this all? You've only brought half a load.' His neck muscles corded, and he jammed a tight fist on his hip. 'Where are your companions, abovegrounder? Where are their supplies?'

Delvina's stomach churned like rocks in the crushing barrels. Nebam was right, they needed more food than this.

The black koraktil's long snout reared up, hot breath fanning Delvina's face. 'They are resting.' Korak's normally friendly voice was as hard and impenetrable as his row of curved teeth. His tail lashed, flattening bushes on the edge of the clearing. 'As I should be.' A puff of smoke wisped from his nostrils.

The morning birdsong and the chatter of the toolwuns waiting to unload the other koraktil fell silent.

Nebam stumbled back a step, holding out his stubby hands, palms outward. 'No offense, Highwun. But a belt can only be tightened so many notches.'

'And a branch can only be bent so far before it breaks.'

The anger leached out of the koraktil's voice until it sounded worn-down, thin, like an over-used file.

He reared up on his haunches and spread out his great wings. Even as his form stretched, it shrank in size to that of a tall human with silvery-white skin, dark-green eyes and flyaway hair as black as obsidian, an older echo of her friend Zadeki's face.

Korak's features seemed gaunter than a few days ago, and his generous mouth flattened into a thin line. He ran a hand over his face. 'That is all my people's food stores, son of Havilah. It will take time to move further along the songlines of the Great Forest to collect more.'

Delvina calmed her breathing. The Forest Folk were friends, but they didn't need to be here helping them. Picking up a clay drinking container of cooled broth and an algae cake set to one side, she handed them to Korak. 'Please, come below, sir, and rest.'

'My thanks, brave Delvina. My very bones are weary.' He lifted the container and drank in one long gulp. Then he nibbled the algae cake, and with a sigh, swallowed it whole like a youngwun swallowing a bitter healing potion. Tension smoothed from his face and a hint of humour returned to his dark eyes. 'And my apologies for my bad temper. It is against the nature of this wild and noble form to be a beast of burden.'

'We are grateful for your help, Highwun,' Thirdwun Danel said.

Delvina nodded. The Thirdwun was right. The food supplies would be all but gone otherwise.

Secondwun Nebam tugged his scrappy ginger beard, a sour look on his narrow face. 'Yes, well, I did not mean to criticise.'

'No doubt, son of Havilah,' Korak said, his eyebrow lifting a fraction. 'We understand that your situation is dire. Where is the Kinleader?'

'In the farm caverns with Matu ... er the Overseer Havilah ... taking stock of the damage to the crops.' Nebam waved his arms, 'I need to check on how the Diamond

North Crew is progressing with the burial niches. The Remembering Ceremony starts at second shift. 'Danel, see these toolwuns stow the supplies in the storage caverns.'

Danel nodded and the toolwuns scrambled to follow Nebam's orders, loading the half-empty paniers onto one of the handcarts.

Nebam gave a satisfied grunt before he spun round and stabbed a blunt finger at Delvina. 'Runner Delvina, take Highwun Korak to the Overseer and stop gaping like a stunned cave fish.'

Delvina's cheeks warmed at his sharp tone. Sometimes Nebam sounded too much like his disgraced brother, Putarn. She stood taller. 'At once, Secondwun.'

He grunted and stumped his way past her and Korak towards the entrance in the Cauldron wall to the tunnels below.

Delvina beckoned to Highwun Korak and headed after Nebam. 'This way, sir.'

The tunnels sloped down, winding their way towards the Great Causeway. Strips of glimmer lights cast a soothing blue glow, and her muscles eased at the familiar constant coolness of the air. Not so long ago these tunnels were forbidden, coated in dust and wreathed with spiderwebs. Now, the floor was scuffed and muddied from the passage of boots and the metal rimmed wheels of the handcarts.

Perhaps in time, they could build glimmer trucks to bring in the supplies. Her stomach squirmed with unease. What if there was no more food from the forest? The perilous journey she and Retza endured to ask the Forest Folk's aid would be for naught.

'There are more ways than one to solve a problem, daughter of the mountain. The Maker will show us a way forward.'

Delvina started at the Adelphi's lilting voice that seemed to echo her thoughts. Maybe he was right. Hadn't everyone insisted scaling the cliffs of the Cauldron would be impossible, yet she and Retza had done it. 'We should be okay, if the farm caverns aren't as badly damaged as the Lead Hand Gregan suspects.'

'Perhaps. Or there may be other ways to find food for your kin.' His stomach growled loud enough for her to hear it, and he rubbed it. 'Do you know where Zadeki is?'

'Your son is with the Kinleader, sir.' A feeling of warmth wrapped around her at the thought of the tall Adelphi, with his infectious smile and exuberant attitude to life. While perhaps not as sturdily built as one of her people like Danel or Nebam, the charming young abovegrounder had proved to be a good friend.

Korak's teeth flashed in a teasing smile, the first she'd seen since he'd landed. 'Ah, good. I hope he hasn't done anything impetuous while I've been away.'

Delvina shook her head. 'No, sir.'

They turned into the Great Causeway. The familiar chuckling sound of the river deep in the central ravine echoed off the stone walls. Despite the glimmer lights, a dense gloom hovered over what was normally a bustling place. The debris had been cleared away and the supply outlets that lined either side of the broad cavern patched with makeshift repairs and boarded closed. There hadn't been time to do more. The bodies were gone, at least, carried to the lower caverns in preparation for burial later today.

Some distance away, a long line of crewless and

crewed snaked its way from the Commissary. Weary mothers, slouched oldbeards and strapping youngwuns shuffled forward in fits and starts with the occasional push as rations were metered out to the head of the line.

'Is that all,' a youngwun old enough to be a Prentice yelled. 'Half a weevily algae cake, a handful of dried mushrooms, and a few fish bones? That's not enough to feed a cave spider.'

An angry murmur ran through the line, whether in support of the youngwun's complaint or in condemnation, Delvina wasn't sure. Her neck hairs prickled. It was hard not to remember the riot in which she and Retza had almost been crushed not that long ago.

The stocky server waved his arm at the youngwun. 'If you want more, then join one of the work crews. Now move it before I call the watchers on you.'

An old woman poked the youngwun with her walking stick. 'Get on with you, we're all just as hungry.'

At first the youngwun bristled, then with a low growl, he pushed his way past her and headed toward the Commons.

'And don't come back for second serve,' the commissioner yelled. 'I'll remember your pretty mug.'

A low rumble of laughter ran through the line, and Delvina relaxed a little. The agitator and bully, Javot, wasn't here to stir things up. With everything that had happened over the last several rosters, maybe she was getting too jittery.

She started when Korak spoke in a low voice. 'Do not all get the same portion?'

'The workwuns get more.'

Some in the line twisted around to stare as they

walked past. Eyes widened, jaws slackened, and a whisper spread down the line. A mother pulled her littlewun closer and an oldwun made a sign to ward off the Dark Ones.

Delvina hoped Korak hadn't seen it. She quickened her pace heading for the nearest arched bridge spanning the central ravine. Deep below the bridge, the blue glimmerlight scattered off the dark rush of water.

'Your people do not seem overjoyed to see me,' Korak said once they'd crossed over and left the stares behind.

Delvina swallowed hard. 'I'm sure they appreciate all you have done for us. It's just that ...' Just that what? Despite the fact that the Forest Folk helped defeat Putarn's rebellion, they were still outsiders, abovegrounders. The realms had been shut off from the outside for over two hundred years. Besides, Korak and his Kin could change into fearsome beasts in an instant. Many had seen their powerful jaguar and koraktil forms and tales of the Kinleader Telsima's transformation into a huge bat had spread like a mine fire in an exposed coal seam. 'Um ...'

'No need to explain, earth's daughter. People are often afraid of the unknown. So it is with our enemies and even, sometimes, our friends.'

They passed the laneway to the Greenstone South Crib, her old crib. Delvina slowed her pace. 'You have enemies?'

Korak's generous mouth twisted into a half-smile. 'Perhaps 'enemies' is too strong a word, but we are not lauded by the Sea Dragon King and his loyal subjects.' He stopped, scanning the area. 'Isn't this the way to the Grand Cavern and the Heart Room? I thought the farms would be elsewhere.'

'The lifts are nearby. We could've taken the stairs, but

the farm caverns are three levels down, close to the river and the waste outlets, so this way is quicker. If you don't mind, sir.' Delvina wondered why this Sea Dragon King, who once ruled the Glittering Realm, hated the Forest Folk.

'The rift with our Vaane cousins is a long story perhaps for another time.' Once more his words mirrored her thoughts. Korak rubbed a hand over his face. 'I am tired. And still ravenous to be honest. Less walking sounds good.'

'We're almost there.'

The outlets on either side were grander as they approached the Old Overseers quarters. To one side a great staircase curved up to the Grand Cavern and the Crystal Heart. Beneath the balcony, four mesh doors covered the openings to shafts down to the lower levels. Toolwuns in jerkins, hats and metalled boots, clumped together in slow-moving groups, ready to start the first shift. Most moved out of their way, though Delvina's shoulder blades itched as curious eyes followed their progress. She approached the watcher in black-bat leather standing near west glimmer lift and tapping his truncheon against his thigh.

'Secondwun Nebam wishes me to take the Highwun Korak to the Overseer in the Farm Caverns, sir.'

The watcher tugged his thick fingers through his blue-dyed beard. His bald head gleamed in the glimmer lights. 'Is that so, Messenger.' His eyes flicked over Korak before turning to the toolwuns from Ferrous East filing into the lift. 'Out you lot. Let the highwun through,' he yelled.

The toolwuns shuffled out, grumbling until meeting the watcher's fierce glare.

Delvina stepped into the cage.

Korak stayed where he was. 'Is that safe?'

'Of course, sir. Accidents rarely happen.'

The watcher spat a thick globule into a bin. 'They say you can fly, abovegrounder. What have you got to worry about?'

Korak laughed, a melodious sound akin to birdsong she'd heard in the forests. 'Going down deep holes into the earth is not to my liking, any more than a winged creature likes a cage.'

But he stepped forward and only took one deep shuddering breath as the wire doors slid shut with a soft clang, and the glimmer winch whirred into action. With a jerk, the cage plummeted downwards. Delvina rolled with the familiar heave of descent.

Korak clutched her shoulder than regained his balance. 'How long?'

'Almost there.'

The cage shuddered to a sudden stop. She stepped out into the long tunnel, the musty smell of mushrooms, lichen and rotted potatoes hitting her like the blast of a furnace.

'It's not far down this corridor. We can take a glimmer truck if you wish.'

The Adelphi shook his head. 'We'll walk, if you don't mind. Tired or not, I think I'd like my feet on solid ground.'

Delvina dipped her head to hide a smile. She led the way down the tunnel.

Zadeki had the exact same reaction the first time he'd taken the lifts. Now he rode them without a twitch and balanced on the rim of the glimmer trucks with carefree bravado. She snuck a look at Korak. Zadeki was very like his father. Despite her people's suspicions, she was sure her confidence in the Forest Folk and their Maker was not misplaced.

Zadeki shortened his stride to Retza's with some difficulty. Glimmer lights, arranged in long strips along the rock roof of the cavern, flooded the huge space with bright light mimicking the golden hue of daylight. Ahead of them, the two leaders, the new Overseer and Kinleader Telsima, walked, heads bent together in conversation and seemingly oblivious to the workers grubbing through black, lumpish soil on either side of the path. Overseer Havilah was short, square and stocky like Retza and indeed most Darane; the Kinleader taller and slender, though still short for the Kin. Both women were forces to be reckoned with.

'Hard to believe that only half a cycle of the silver moon ago the plants were flourishing,' Retza muttered to Zadeki.

Zadeki took a breath to speak and gagged on the odours of black mildew and rot.

If these were the Darane farm caverns, they were a sorry sight indeed. Though, it was a wonder anything could grow this deep beneath the weight of rock, dirt and ice towering over their heads. Withered stalks stuck straight up like tiny stilted trees seared by lightning. An occasional plant retained drooping leaves, sickly yellow and leached-out green at the serrated edges.

Zadeki nudged Retza. 'So, you eat the leaves?'

'No, of course not. The poison in the leaves will give you a bellyache.' Retza bent down, pulled up a withered plant and prised bulbous lumps from the thicket of roots—some purple-green, some black and shrivelled. 'We eat the roots. We also have caverns with mushroom farms and algae pools.'

'Have they wilted too?'

'They have less need for the glimmer lights, so weren't as badly affected when the Crystal Heart failed.' Retza freed one of the bigger round lumps and threw it to him.

Zadeki snatched it from the air, and brushed the dirt off the purplish-green skin. His stomach, as hollow as a rotten tree stump, grumbled at the thought of food. He hadn't been truly full since returning with Delvina and Retza to the Underground Realm to help save the Glimmer Heart. On impulse, he took a bite. Tart bitterness assaulted his mouth and forced tears from his eyes.

'Eeeyew.' He spat the root out. 'How can you eat that, earthbiter? It's foul.'

Retza tipped his head back and roared, his laughter echoing off the cavern walls, earning a reproving glance from the Overseer and stares from those tending the fields. 'You cook them first, above-grounder.' He added in a more subdued tone.

Zadeki scrubbed his tongue, his face wrinkling. 'That I can agree on.'

Now he thought of it, there were roots in the forest that needed careful processing to be edible. And sava root was much better roasted on the dampened-down coals with fresh river fish. His mouth watered at the thought and he pressed a hand against his stomach. He at least could leave these benighted tunnels and, with a simple shape change, fly out and across the jagged mountains to the green bounty of the Great Forest. The situation was more dire for his new-found friends. For them, the only way out was scaling the vertical walls of the Cauldron and crossing the mountains against the forces of snow, ice and wind.

Havilah and the Kinleader stopped once level with the Darane who were sorting through the heaps of dug-up roots at the other end of the cavern. The piles of withered plants and blackened roots were many times higher than the pile of salvaged potatoes in the barrels. Zadeki and Retza stopped a few paces behind the women.

Kinleader Telsima turned around in a half-circle, taking in the cavern, her eyes dark with concern. 'Are all the food caverns like this?'

Havilah bowed her grey streaked head. 'Most of the potato farms are worse. The glimmer lights were weak many shifts before failing completely. Restoring the Crystal Heart has not been enough to save them.' She beckoned to an older Darane with a hunched back and long mossy beard.

The toolwun dipped his head and hurried over. 'Your honour,' he said in an overloud voice.

'What is your assessment, Lead Hand Gregan?'

He rubbed his beard and looked askance at the Kinleader. 'As much as four-fifths of the crops have been destroyed, including the Overseer's fish stocks.

Havilah pointed to the barrel, half full of small, wrinkled roots. 'But you can reseed from the root stocks.'

'Yeah-ah. Though the blight has soured the soil in the outer caverns.' The squat man stared at his mud-stained boots, his grey eyebrows bristling. 'Even once we plant, it'll take over five rosters—one hundred days—before they're truly ready to harvest.'

'I see,' Havilah said. She seemed to shrink a little. 'We are grateful for the food you've supplied, Kinleader Telsima. It would seem we need to depend on your generosity a little longer, until the first harvest.'

'If you call that food,' Gregan muttered under his hand, as though he thought his words unheard. He glanced up at the Kinleader.

'Could you grow your crops in the Cauldron?' Zadeki asked.

'Dim-witted idea. My workwuns would be burned to a crisp. The plants too,' Gregan muttered.

Zadeki's cheeks flamed. He was only trying to help. Da-matu placed a light hand on his shoulder.

'Thank you, Lead Hand Gregan.' Havilah murmured. 'Keep me informed of progress.'

'Yes, your honour.' Gregan darted a sideways look at Zadeki before stumping off towards the others working the farm.

Retza growled. 'It's not so stupid an idea. We could work at night. Or we could bring soil from outside.'

'Tamrak's children in the mountains to the north grow potatoes as high—' the Kinleader paused and eyes focused on the other end of the cavern. Zadeki tilted his head to listen.

Hurried footsteps echoed from the tunnel beyond and moments later Delvina's short figure in jerkin and breeches emerged between the rough arched door. She jogged toward them, followed by a figure close to twice as tall, his lithe figure wrapped in a white sarum.

Zadeki grinned. His father was back from the supply flight, but there was a slight stumble in Baba's walk. That wasn't so good. Baba was pushing himself past safe limits with too many trips and shape changes. If only he could help him more, but the koraktil shape was beyond his present ability. In fact, few of his kin had grasped it.

Delvina drew level to Zadeki and her pale-grey eyes

caught his. Her broad face crinkled into a warm smile. Zadeki smiled back at his plucky friend and, beside him, Retza cracked a rare grin. These two were his friends no matter what the future brought.

'Youngest son, good to see you,' Baba grasped Zadeki's shoulder, his hand heavy as he rested a portion of his weight on him. His strong presence carried the scent of open air, sunlight on green leaves and a sense of home. Zadeki curbed the sudden ache to see the sky, the urge to leave this place that smelled of death. Yet, how could he think of his own comfort when his friends were still in danger? He had promised to help them, and he would.

Delvina dipped her head. 'Highwun Korak has come with the latest supplies, Overseer.'

'You are welcome, Korak.' Havilah looked past him to the empty pathway. 'Are your companions resting?'

'Yes, Daughter of the Mountain. They rest with our Kin in the Forest.'

'You looked stretched thin, son of my son.'

Baba turned to the Kinleader. 'Da-Matu. Bad news. Sudden rains mean the sava root harvest has ended sooner than we expected. We will need to move further into the Great Forest for more food both for our little ones and our mountain dwelling friends.'

Havilah's forehead creased into new lines. 'What are you saying? You have no more food for us?'

'We have no need of stone-built storehouses or hoarded food which rots and withers with rains or are too heavy to carry as we walk the land,' the Kinleader said. 'As the Maker wills, we will gather more when the land replenishes. But it will take time.'

Havilah's chin jutted out and her face hardened. 'Time my people don't have. You heard my Lead Hand of the Farming Crews. Without more food, my people will die. Can they not look harder?'

'They already have. This is a heavy burden on my people. We cannot conjure food from the forest, earth-sister, any more than you could conjure it from the stone walls.'

The leaders locked eyes, grey-green challenging amethyst, the easy camaraderie between them shed like an entangling garment.

Zadeki's muscles tensed as the air seemed to crackle. Somewhere close, water dripped with a steady plink, plink.

Havilah threw up her arms. 'What are we to do?'

'The supplies we have brought should last you a few ten-days, at least. By the Maker's grace, we have given you time to find other ways to survive. Find a way outside, seek a new way of life, trade with the Tamrak's—'

'The caverns are our life. The Gates are shut fast against us. What we need is food to last until the potato harvest.'

A long mournful gong resounded throughout the cavern.

Zadeki's arms prickled with alarm. 'Are you under attack?'

The Overseer sighed, her shoulder slumping. 'No, it's the reminder—an hour before the Remembering ceremony for our dead. For now, I must prepare. Runners Retza and Delvina, find Scrybe Barekia and assist her in attending the ceremony.' She took a few steps and stopped. 'Kinleader Telsima, please do not think us ungrateful. Without your help our realm would already be lost.'

The Kinleader took Havilah's hands in her own. 'Let us stand with you as you bury your dead. And then we will find the way ahead.'

Havilah's eyes softened. 'I hope so. Your support is welcome.'

Zadeki relaxed his stance, glad that tensions had eased for now. He hoped solutions would be found, for the sake of the twins and their kin. Whatever happened, the earthbiters faced hard choices.

Lady Zara folded her arms and tapped her foot on the stone floor. This was just not good enough! Ever since her father had been ousted by Havilah and her cronies, she and her younger brother Jesson had been hustled from one confinement to another. At least this cavern, which housed the last remaining Crystal Heart, was spacious.

The high stone roof arched over their heads. In the centre a bunch of glowing Heart crystals angled out from the base like Jesson's stick-up hair. Glimmer crystals higher than the tallest toolwun, higher than even the Adelphi, their faceted surfaces pulsing with a blue-green light.

The old Scrybe, Barekia, sat on a stool at the base of the Crystal Heart, her knotted fingers busy tinkering with the dials and knobs on the control panel. A bandage slipped over her forehead, from her injury when Havilah's rebel son, Putarn, had knocked the oldwun to the ground while threatening to kill Jesson. Not that the rebels' internal conflicts were Zara's concern, unless she could somehow use them to return the Glittering Realms to the rightful Overseer, her father.

Zara's eyes were drawn past the bowed head of the old woman, back to the soft pulsating glow of the Heart. She pulled at the teardrop pendant on her chest, its familiar shape giving a sense of connection with her mother and father and her life before all this. She could almost imagine a high-pitched ringing, just beyond the edge of hearing, as though the Heart crystals sang to her of life and power. She felt the tendrils of possibilities snaking out from this cavern, winding their way through to the cribs, the creches, the Causeway and the storerooms, going wide and deep. And if she could control it, perhaps ... She took a step closer to the Heart, the teardrop warm beneath her fingers.

'I'm hungry, Zara.' A tug on her skirt and Jesson's piping voice shattered her focus. Zara dropped her hand and shivered, suddenly conscious of her own empty belly. The meal at first shift felt a long time ago.

'Soon, Jesson.' She patted her brother's back. 'We need to wait.'

Her elegant shoulders drooped, and she pulled at the fraying border of her sleeve. Waiting was all they seemed to do these days. Wait for food. Wait to learn their fate. Wait for Baba to return and take back the realm.

There was nothing to do, nowhere to go, no one to talk to. She was bored to the point of screaming. She itched to turn over furniture, to make a crash and bang and startle the smug expressions off the faces of the watchers guarding the newly repaired door.

She didn't recognise these two. They were the traitor Gilarth's stooges anyway. Head Watcher Gilarth now. Baba had trusted him to guard Jesson. Instead, he was helping Havilah, no doubt to advance himself. She gritted her teeth. He should've helped them escape.

Jesson tugged at her sleeve. 'I don't want to wait, Zara.'

'I know.' She turned and ruffled her small brother's pale golden hair. 'The watchers will bring us food sooner or later.'

A gong sounded, a low foreboding sound.

Jesson jumped up and down. 'Does that mean they'll bring food now?'

'No, I don't think so.' It wasn't the normal signal for change of shifts. Zara pulled Jesson closer. What disaster now? The guards stood straighter but didn't rush toward her, or out to the Great Cavern. Old Scrybe Barekia didn't even blink, she was so focused on her tinkering.

'Ow!.' Jesson wriggled out from her grip, clutching his splinted arm.

'Is it hurting.'

'Only a little, Za-za. You squeezed it.' He jiggled up and down. 'Can I see what the Scrybe is doing?'

Zara's throat tightened. The old woman was harmless enough, but her instinct was to keep the rebels at a distance and her brother close. Still, perhaps she could learn more about the crystals.

'Zara? Can I? Can I? Pleeease.'

'Very well. Let's see what she is up too, then.'

Barekia was bent almost in half, fiddling with a lever and muttering something under her breath. She looked up as they got near, her creased face breaking into a gap-toothed smile. 'Ah, youngwuns. What can I do for you?'

Zara assumed a nonchalant air. 'What are you doing?'

'Cleaning the intake valves and adjusting the whatsit thingy ....' The words blurred together in a meaningless jumble.

'Do you know how this works?' Jesson asked, his eyes as round as the dials on the bronze control panel.

Zara snorted. 'Baba said the working of the Crystal Heart was as mysterious as a woman's heart.' Matu had always smiled at that quip.

'Spoken like a man.' Barekia chuckled, her face

creasing into a thousand more wrinkles. 'As my baba would say, the Crystal Heart is like an underground river, you can't tame it, but you can guide it with a little ingenuity.'

Zara sneered. 'And how would a toolwun know more than my baba, Overseer of the Glittering Realms, son of Hezikah?'

Barekia spread out her hands. 'My baba was a techwun, a special toolwun who cared for the Heart before the Old Overseer mur...' Barekia's eyes hardened, before softening in memory again. 'My baba knew a thing or two, though I was more interested in being a Scrybe like my matu than a techwun ...'

Zara smirked. 'So, you really don't know what you're doing, oldwun.'

'She got the Heart working, didn't she?'

Zara jumped at the gruff voice and spun around. Prentice Retza stood behind them, feet apart and hand on the copper messenger cylinder tucked through his belt. Retza's twin sister, Delvina hovered behind him with her kind grey eyes and shy smile.

Retza glanced at Zara and quickly looked away, his cheeks reddening. He had strong hands and there was something solid about his stance. For a lowwun, he wasn't so bad looking and he'd kept calm in the crisis, like when Putarn had wanted to hurt Jesson. Among all the rebels, she liked these two the most.

Barekia put down her wrench and cracked her frail knuckles. 'I did get it working, though Lady Zara got it going the second time.' She peered at the two new arrivals. 'So what mischief are you youngwuns up to?'

Zara folded her arms over the thump-thump of her heart. 'My father would know what to do.'

The others exchanged glances and a look of pity stole over the old woman's face. 'If he still lives.'

A tremor passed through Zara. He was alive, he had to be. Yet why had the Glimmer Heart faded if he still lived, only to be brought to life by her touch? Perhaps, he was beyond the crystal's reach, somewhere safe to plan how to restore things to the way they should be. Another less welcome voice whispered inside. He would demand sacrifices, he would punish these prentices, and perhaps he'd be angry at her for not bringing Jesson to him sooner, for allowing his son's capture. Hadn't Baba insisted that the blood of the prentices was necessary to appease the Dark Ones. Zara shook her head as if to dislodge rock grit from her hair. Her baba had acted as he did for good reason. Despite their virtuous intentions, Havilah and the twins had brought chaos to the Underground Realm.

Delvina brushed her ash-blonde fringe out of her eyes. 'Please, let's not argue. Not now, not this shift.' She took Barekia's hand. 'Highwun, it's time to get ready. Overseer Havilah sent us to fetch you for the Remembering Ceremony.'

Zara's pulse fluttered, the memory of the corpses scattered in the Grand Cavern and Heart Room following Putarn's rebellion against his mother, Havilah. Rebels fighting among themselves.

'Can we come,' Jesson asked, his face solemn.

Retza chewed his lip. 'Ah...' He glanced at his twin sister's troubled face. 'We could ask—

'No need to take the trouble,' Zara snapped, her cheeks burning. For all she had helped them, they still treated her as the enemy. 'We will be comfortable right here.' She turned away as Jesson's face crumpled.

'Perhaps it's for the best, youngwun,' Barekia said. 'Many died under your father's rule and too often grief and anger need a focus.'

Zara flinched, as though the oldwun had slapped her in the face. And how many died under Havilah's son, Putarn's rebellion?

'As you wish,' she said, her voice congealed into ice. 'Come Jesson.'

She turned and marched back to her allotted alcove, pulling Jesson with her. What was the point of arguing with these lowwuns. True, they had saved Jesson, protected her twice now when they didn't have to, but they did not care about her and her brother. How could they? At least, the rebels needed her connection to the Crystal Heart. It would buy her time, time to find a way to escape. She and Jesson would find Baba, and things would return to normal. She touched her pendant. She knew Baba still lived.

The smooth rock walls pressed in on Zadeki, the cavern's air still and muggy and rank with the smell of people jammed close together. Only a faint puff of new air came from the ventilation shafts high in the cobwebbed roof. This deep cavern, long and wide, twenty levels down, was not made any fresher by the smell of incense and candle smoke curling in the dust-laced air.

Black angular openings carved deep into the rock walls on two opposing sides gave the appearance of lidless eyes watching his every move. Further along, statues of bearded Darane were carved in the living rock and the older, bricked-in niches faded into the darkness beyond the flickering torchlight. Like the sunken temple, this space wasn't lit by the ever-present glimmer lights.

Baba leaned into Zadeki, an indication of his father's deep weariness.

'Perhaps you should have slept instead of coming to the ceremony, Baba, and got something to eat,' he whispered. 'Havilah would've understood.'

Baba's lips quirked one-sided. 'Eat what exactly. I can hardly wolf down half the stores I've flown in. I'll be fine. There will be time for sleep after this, and it is important to honour these dwellers of the deep's passing. Besides, Da-matu would like us to gauge the mood. Keep your eyes sharp and your senses alert.'

Zadeki nodded and scanned the squat sturdy figures in front of them, filling the space and spilling into spare corners. Their deep sorrow seemed to pulse through the air. The Kinleader had chosen to join the Overseer Havilah standing near the first of the newly opened burial niches. Havilah's new Secondwun and son, Nebam, stood on one side, legs astride and hands hooked into his belt, sparse beard thrust forward. Taller and thinner than most Darane, Danel was on the other side, the long staff of the speaker in one hand. Watchers in black bat leather guarded the entrances and were scattered around the edges of the crowd.

In front of the leadwuns were the bodies, Zadeki counted fifty-six. Most were the length of Darane adults, some could only be younglings, laying on matting in two neat rows and dressed in white and jewels. Grieving family or cribmates knelt or crouched beside them, pulling beards or plaited hair in anguish.

'It's as though they have no hope beyond the grave,' Zadeki murmured.

Death happened rarely among his people. Except for

accident or foul play, they lived far beyond the short years of the younger races or even the Darane. And if death came, in its time or out of it, it was a continuation of the journey to the world beyond the veil.

'Perhaps, in their worship of the Dark Ones, Darian's children forgot the Maker's promises,' Baba murmured.

The shuffle of boots near the entrance caught Zadeki's attention. Delvina stepped into the cavern, her long pale plait swinging down her back. Retza followed, his face solemn. Standing on his toes, Zadeki could see the top of a bent white head bobbing between them.

Retza pushed his way through the toolwuns, clearing a path until the trio reached Havilah. The twins melted to one side, revealing the stooped and frail figure of Scrybe Barekia in a long white robe and clutching a book to her chest.

Thirdwun Danel stepped forward and thumped down the Speaker's pole on the floor, the sound echoing like distant thunder rolling across the tops of the trees in the Great Forest. The sting of rain on his face would be more than a welcome change from these dark caverns. Around him, the subdued hum of conversation faded away to a soft shuffling of feet and an occasional cough.

'Where's the priest?' a gruff voice demanded, close by.

'Gone with Overseer Uzza,' someone muttered in front of them before being shushed by a companion. The crowd was tense, an undercurrent of fear and uncertainty scenting the air.

'Silence, the Overseer Havilah speaks.' Danel gave the staff a final hard thump.

Havilah stood forward, the orange light of the torches burnishing her medallion of office to orange fire. Dressed in formal robes, she held out her hands, eyes like purple jewels in a face of sculptured stone. 'Scrybe Barekia, who restored the Heart for us, will speak the old prayers and lead us in remembrance of our fallen.'

Barekia lifted and opened the ancient codex, but barely glanced at it. 'Great One, hear us today ...

'Struck down by her own grandson, Putarn,' someone hissed behind a hand. 'Where's he now?'

'Confined in the holding cells.'

'As bad as Uzza. Someone should have thrown that slag heap off a cliff by now,' another mumbled.

'Course not. He's her son. If she protects Uzza's brats, she's going to protect her own.'

'Maybe that's a good thing. We were better off before.'

'Be quiet,' an old woman hissed. 'Have you no respect.'

'Yes, shush. And she has those demon beasts—' the toolwun gave a hasty glance over his shoulder and snagged Zadeki's eyes. Face ashen, the man looked away and he shuffled forward.

Barekia's voice grew stronger the more she spoke. 'Too many have died defending us against the chaos, against ignorance and greed. Each death diminishes us. Only together can we stand against the darkness, our hearts and our hands joined. Our troubles are not yet over, but despite it all, the Crystal Heart beats in the Heart Room, giving light and power. By the Maker's favour, the Great One, we will prevail, and the memories of the fallen will not be lost. Together we speak their names and ask that they find solace and haven beyond death's door.'

Danel brought down the speaker's staff. 'Step forward and speak their names.'

The Lead Hand beside the furthest body stood up, 'Nabur, Thirdwun of the Copper East Crew, son of Baylor and Neeia.'

Another stood, 'Andri, toolwun of Silver West.

'Leah, carewun of East creche ...

The names rolled forth like the rumbling song of the underground river, one after the other. Friends and families pressed close to many of the fallen, and when the last name had been spoken, Barekia called out, 'We will not forget them,' and all the Darane roared in assent.

Then one by one, the bodies were lifted and placed in the niches with trinkets or a favoured tool. Toolwuns sealed the openings with round stones.

A soft many-throated sigh shivered through the crowd. Some bowed their heads with quiet weeping while others stood with stoic faces. Zadeki wiped the tears dripping off his face. Without solutions, more of Delvina and Retza's people would die. They had already lost too much.

Danel thumped the staff three times. 'The Overseer provides food and drink in honour of the fallen in the Grand Cavern.'

'For leadwuns,' someone close by mumbled.

'All are invited, the grieving families and cribs and creches, for leadwuns, crews, and crewless.'

The Darane shuffled toward the entrance in tight clusters, gripping arms and comforting each other.

'What now, Baba?' Zadeki asked, his voice husky. 'Should we join them?'

'Let's wait for the Kinleader.'

Da-Matu embraced Havilah, holding the other leader tight. With a few soft words, she released her and then walked towards Zadeki and Baba. The remaining Darane moved out of her way like leaves before a storm-wind.

Her grey-green gaze swept over Baba and she brushed his arm. 'Korak, son of my son, you need to rest.'

Baba nodded, though Zadeki could see the

reservation in his dark eyes. 'I'll rest better once back in the Forest. I sense that not all welcome us here.'

Havilah walked toward the entrance, head bent in a whispered conversation with the tall watcher, Gilarth, her hand on Nebam on the other side. Danel and the twins followed behind.

'One in the crowd called us monsters,' Zadeki said, finding it hard to keep the puzzlement out of his voice. 'Yet without us ... We gave them our sava harvest ...' His voice faded. Why would his Kin be resented?

At that moment, Delvina glanced up from where she and Retza trailed Havilah and beamed a smile through her tears. He relaxed and waved back. Kind and generous, Delvina's friendship was one thing he could depend on.

'They do well to fear us, though we mean them no harm,' Da-Matu said.

'Yes, but we are three and they are many,' Baba added. 'Perhaps it is time for us to leave.'

'Perhaps, but for now Havilah has invited us to join in this remembrance feast in honour of the fallen. Come!'

Da-Matu increased her pace, soon catching up to where Havilah and the others were making their way out to lifts and the higher levels. Zadeki and Korak followed. As they ducked under the arched doorway, Zadeki looked back at the cavern lit with spluttering torchlight. A dense darkness seemed to coil around the vaulted roof, like the tattered dregs of dark dreams.

Retza slipped through the clumps and knots of grieving people, Delvina close behind him. Leadwuns, toolwuns, crewless and youngwuns filled the Grand Cavern.

Fewer than before the Glimmer Lights first began to fail. Too many had died, and more would follow if the Overseer and the leadwuns didn't find answers soon. Despite Barekia's inspiring words, the air was thick with the scent of tear-soaked felt, stale incense and despair.

Havilah made her way to a raised chair in the centre of a hastily erected podium. Workwuns put up trestles, while others brought in bowls and platters of food, and barrels of drink. Youngwuns trailed the servers or jostled against the tables, their eyes wide and small tongues licking lips. Now the adults were crowding in, some shoving to get closer to the food.

Retza sniffed the air, inhaling enticing aromas of fish, roasted fern root and mushrooms. His stomach rumbled, and he drifted towards the table when Delvina caught his arm.

Head Watcher Gilarth, flanked by two other watchers, moved in. 'Step back. There'll be enough for all. Let's not disrespect the fallen.'

'We could join the other runners,' Delvina said.

Retza swallowed and nodded at Delvina, embarrassed he'd allowed his hunger to lead him. He headed to where the other messengers huddled at a discrete distance from the podium, ready to be summoned if required. The squash of bodies lessened the closer they approached the area under the Old Overseer's balcony.

'How can we spare so much food, when there is so little left in the stores,' Delvina muttered.

After so many days of short rations, Retza wasn't sure he cared, but his sister had a point. He blinked away the memory of the rank potato caverns with their blighted plants.

'The Overseer must know what she's doing.'

'She does indeed.' Retza jumped at Danel's voice coming from the trestle beside him. 'We've tightened our belts notch after notch after notch. And a day or two won't matter once ... if the food runs out.' The Thirdwun sat at a trestle table close to the dais.

Delvina stopped walking and lifted her chin. 'It might make all the difference.'

Danel spread his hands. 'The Overseer sees it differently, Runner, as a matter of morale. Won't matter how many stores we have if the people lose hope or riot.'

'As you say, sir.' Retza gripped Delvina's arm, steering her away from trouble. Never a good idea to argue with the highwuns, but his sister was like that if she thought there was a need.

Danel stood up and waved them over. 'There's a couple of empty spots here, if you wish to join me.'

Retza gaped at the Thirdwun. As Havilah's nephew, Thirdwun and Speaker, it was easy to forget that Danel was not that much older than they were, that they'd been crewmates in Greenstone South before the changes. Even so, the gap between a prentice, like Delvina and he, and Havilah's Speaker felt as deep as the ravine in the Causeway.

Delvina looked as puzzled as he felt. 'But aren't you at the head table with Overseer Havilah?'

Danel scratched his beard. 'It's a little crowded.'

He pointed to where the lead hands of the crews were jostling for a place along the Overseer's table, some sending disgruntled looks when the Kinleader was given a seat beside Havilah. Around the room people were mostly congregating into their crews, though the youngwuns from the creches joined their families for this special occasion. Even the messengers were scattering to sit with parents or siblings. Since their grandfather's death a few solars ago, Delvina was all the family Retza had left. A place next to Danel was as good as any.

He glanced at his twin and nodded. 'Sure. Thanks.'

'Yeah, thanks.'

Then Delvina's face lit up. She jumped and waved to someone near the doors. A tall someone. Zadeki flashed an ever-ready grin at them and hastened toward them, pulling Highwun Korak along with him.

'Do we have room for two more?' Delvina asked.

Danel smiled, lips tight. 'Of course, where would we be without the gallant Forest Folk.'

Which was true enough, as far as it went. So why did Danel seem annoyed at the intrusion?

Danel pulled out the stool next to him for Delvina. Retza took the place opposite his sister, while Zadeki and Korak sat on either side of him. Before Retza could think of something to fill the awkward silence, a server placed a tray loaded with food in front of them.

For a long while everyone's attention was on the delicious treats, even the abovegrounders tucked in with gusto. This was truly a feast long denied. There was food here Retza couldn't even remember eating before, pickled birds' eggs, nest soup, steamed cavecrays, waterweed in some kind of sauce, smoked fish.

After a while those who knew the fallen took turns in standing and telling some exploit or achievement, some funny incident, some endearing moment to the cheers and encouragement and toasts of their cribmates.

Retza's stomach grew tighter with each succulent morsel. He hadn't been this full since eating in the forest with Zadeki and his kin, though surely there was just a little bit more room. He licked his lips and pulled a roasted cave bird toward him and pulled it apart. He offered half to Zadeki, then felt his cheeks warm. The first time he'd met Zadeki, the abovegrounder was in bird form looking a lot like a large prospective meal.

'Do you eat bird?'

Zadeki let out a melodious laugh, his dark eyes crammed full of laughter. It was as though the shapeshifter could read Retza's thoughts.

'Such a tiny thing, it's barely a mouthful. You eat it, earthbiter.' Zadeki glanced at his father. 'Should I get you something more, Baba?'

Korak's dark eyes were thoughtful. 'This is indeed a treat after algae cakes and half-filled bowls of thin mushroom gruel.' He scooped up a handful of toasted and shredded fern root and leant back, tipping the stool, and looked straight at Danel. 'I thought you were running out of food.'

'Better to keep that thought quiet, if you would.' Danel picked his teeth and belched in appreciation of a fine meal. 'This is the last of the Old Overseer's stored delicacies. Rather than keep it for herself or risk bruised egos about who deserved what, Havilah decided to give a feast for all our people in honour of our dead.'

For a moment no one spoke, until Delvina sat straighter. 'It gives us hope while we look for solutions.'

People were talking, or even laughing, together in small groups. Only the tight huddle of crewless in one corner still wore scowls. Despite the grief, the tears at the lost, it had been a long time since his people had been so free of fear and worry. For this night at least.

Retza pushed his plate away and yawned. 'Maybe it's not so crazy.'

'Perhaps. Your leader is wise for her years,' Korak said.

Which was funny, for even though he was Zadeki's baba, he looked far younger than Havilah, with his unlined silvery-white skin and coal-black hair.

Somewhere from the back of the cavern, a toolwun tuned his harp. Two trestles across, someone else brought out her horn, another began wielding a shaker to the rhythm of a familiar tune. First one lone voice and soon, one after another, all that remained awake. After a while, the two abovegrounders joined in, their voices winging higher and weaving in and out of the deep drone of his people in intricate harmonies. When they sang, he could believe the Forest Folk were angels.

As the song at last died away, tight groups left the Grand Cavern for their cribs. Others lay face down on the board or slumped to one side, drooling or snoring gently. Even the ever-present watchers seemed drowsy or melted away. Servers cleared tables of empty dishes and mopped up spills. The celebration was coming to an end.

Retza tapped his sister's arm as he smothered another yawn. 'Shall we go, Del? I've got duty first shift.' And that would only be hours away, so late had they feasted.

'I guess.' She turned to Zadeki and Korak. 'I haven't asked. Where will you sleep?'

'We've built some shelters in the Cauldron, though maybe the Causeway near the Ravine would be sufficient for tonight.' Korak sighed, his face suddenly heavy with denied rest. 'I think I could sleep a week, now we've truly eaten.'

Retza clapped Zadeki on the shoulder. 'There are worse places to sleep. Good night then.' Though there was no accounting for abovegrounder taste. For who would sleep rough when there was comfortable bunk available?

Danel stood up, a little unsteady on his feet, 'Come, I'll

walk with you, Runner Delvina. At least to the junction.'

Smothering a third yawn, Retza linked arms with Delvina and followed Thirdwun Danel in the direction of his bunk and sleep.

Zadeki stepped aside to allow Danel and the twins to move past him. He watched his friends head for the doorway leading to the western wing.

'Go with them if you like.' Baba wobbled and caught the table for support.

'That's alright, Baba.' He hadn't spent a lot of time with the twins over the last few days, but he wasn't keen on leaving Baba to fare for himself when he needed to rest so badly. Constant shapeshifting sapped one's energy, if not restored, and the koraktil form was particularly difficult and demanding. 'We could sleep here.'

'The Causeway has a less closed-in feeling. If you close your eyes, and with the sound of the river, I could almost imagine I was outside these closed-in tunnels.'

Baba set out toward the entrance to the lower levels. With a final glance at his friends, Zadeki followed.

A flicker of a dark shadow caught his eye and his skin hairs prickled. He looked behind him but saw nothing but servers clearing the tables, snoring toolwuns and a knot of what appeared to be crewless and younglings in the corner of the room. It was true what Delvina said, the dread that had crackled through the air of the tunnels had subsided with a good meal and the sharing of grief through stories and song. But something still seemed out of kilter.

With a half-shrug, Zadeki strode on to catch up with his father. They were halfway to the entrance, when the crash of a trestle toppling over reverberated through the room. Zadeki spun toward the source of the commotion, nerves suddenly tingling with the urge to change into a defensive form. The trestle in the corner was turned on its side, the crewless crouching behind it.

Baba grabbed his arm. 'Keep going.'

Even as Zadeki turned again, something splatted on his cheek bone. He wiped the greasy mess of food off with his hand.

A low hiss came from the back of the corner. 'The abovegrounders are holding back from us.'

'Yeah, their cities and caverns must be full of good food.'

'Yet all they bring us is roots and berries.'

'Like cave rats guarding their store holes.'

The words were slurred, the sounds a bit jumbled, but there was no mistaking the tone, aggressive, angry. Zadeki pulled against Baba's grip pulling him to the door.

'Jazadek, son of my heart, stay grounded. Remember who and what you are.'

A growl rumbled deep in Zadeki's chest. How could Baba be so calm? After all they'd done to help, all they'd risked when they could have walked away, all of it dismissed as so much trash. It wasn't as if they had storerooms, they didn't need them.

His throat burned, and his heart contracted as the urge to take on the jaguar form sang through him like a fire ravaging the forest in drought.

'We've given you all the food we could spare. Should we starve our little ones because of your foolishness?' His words bounced off stone walls.

A sudden hush settled over the room, accentuated by the heavy breathing of the crewless and the creak of a stool. No one spoke. There were six of them, a few half-grown, all mostly skin and bone. Not a threat, not really.

Behind him the slither of skidding boots on stone as the few remaining Darane fled the room.

'Come, youngest son,' Baba's voice was more a breath of wind than sound. 'They want a fight, but we don't have to give them one.'

Zadeki rubbed the seep of blood off his cheek and allowed Baba's solid presence to calm him. 'Maybe I could just shake them a little. I don't need to bite them.'

'Tempting.' Baba choked off a low laugh. 'But hard to explain to Havilah or the Kinleader.'

Bootsteps resounded in the corridors outside. Gilarth burst into the room from the main entry at the same time as the twins and Danel ran through the other doorway.

'What's the problem,' the tall watcher demanded, his eyes darting between them and the riff-raff in the corner.

'No problem,' Baba answered. 'Your friends seem to have tipped the trestle over in their haste to be ... helpful.'

'Humph.' Gilarth grunted. He bent and picked up the cracked bowl rolling at Zadeki's feet. His iron-grey gaze swept around the room. 'Well I will assist them to a secure place to sleep tonight. Would you like an escort to the rooms the Overseer provided, Highwun?'

'Thanks for the offer, but no, we'll be fine,' Baba said.

Gilarth stroked his trimmed beard. 'As you wish, Highwun.' He beckoned to Retza, his eyes not moving from the group at the back. 'Retza, give me a hand with this rabble, since my watchers seem to be dozing or taking their pleasures elsewhere, forgetting their duties.'

Retza blinked. 'Ah, I ...'

'We can help,' Zadeki offered. The rabble as Gilarth called them were still restless and ready for a fight.

Gilarth shook his head. 'No, go with your father, lad. Retza will help.'

'I can take your shift in the morning, Retza.' Delvina patted her twin's back. Her gaze snagged Zadeki's. 'Danel and I will show you the rooms the Overseer set aside for you.'

Baba stood straighter. 'Perhaps, for one night.'

Danel quickly replaced a frown with a polite smile. 'Of course.' He nodded at Gilarth. 'Thanks for taking the matter in hand, Head Watcher. If you feel able to handle it?'

The big Darane waved them away.

Zadeki felt the rest of the tension leave his muscles. Delvina welcomed their presence, but it was becoming obvious that not everyone wanted them here. But tonight, Baba needed sleep.

'**Retza, catch.**' Gilarth threw a baton.

With a grunt of surprise, Retza reached out and caught it before it slammed into him.

Delvina and the Forest Folk disappeared into the tunnels leading to the western quarter. Even the erstwhile sleepers had made themselves scarce. They were alone in the Grand Cavern. and still no watchers at the doors to back them up.

The bunch of gormless crewless huddled behind the tipped-up trestle, the biggest of the louts sizing up Gilarth, then eyes sidling towards Retza, no doubt assessing the odds, two against six. He understood why Gilarth had drafted him, but having Danel, Delvina and the Forest Folk would have made rounding up the troublemakers much easier.

'So you lot coming hard or easy?' Gilarth growled.

'We're staying here. We weren't doing anything,' one yelled.

'Then step out here one by one so Retza can search for weapons.'

Gilarth's offer was met with stony silence. He grinned, sudden and fierce. 'Right, thought so. Retza, you go left, I'll go right.'

Taking a deep breath, Retza gripped the truncheon, surprised at how the handle fitted snug in his palm. Perhaps not his trusty lift-bar, but it would do the job against this lot. He gave it a few practice swings and mirrored Gilarth's movements.

Gilarth cracked his whip, the tip flicking within ninas of the group's heads. The crewless ducked and the bluster melted from the faces of younger ones. The smallest made a dash past Retza for the entryway. Retza grabbed his arm and pinned him with the truncheon.

'I didn't do nothing,' the youngwun whined, his mushroom-grey eyes wide with mock innocence.

Retza prised the lump of cave rock from the lad's other hand. 'No need for this, then.'

Gilarth looked across from bashing the two biggest heads together. 'Yeah, you did, young Darin. You kept bad company if nothing else. Time you learnt to keep out of trouble.' He hauled the two dazed captives out. 'Make yourself useful and tie these two up.'

Darin gulped then nodded. Once Retza released him, he looped rope around first one, then the second, while Retza checked the knots. Two others cowered back into the corner, hands held up in surrender. The sixth, a scrawny lout with a thick beard and pointy nose, hadn't moved, though his gaze darted between Retza and

Gilarth. His face was familiar, a friend of Javot's, though his name eluded Retza.

'Alright, you three, file out from behind the trestle and Darin here will secure you.' Gilarth flicked his whip. 'Be quick about it. Retza, keep an eye on them.'

The closest one obeyed, his buddy shuffling after him. They allowed Darin to tie them to the other two.

'Why you taking us in? We were just having a little fun,' spat pointy nose. Fenna, that was his name.

Retza's stomach tightened with sudden unease. Fenna whipped his hand from under the table and something flashed in the glimmerlight.

Retza lept forward and brought the truncheon down on Fenna's wrist with a solid crunch. He yelped, and a rusted iron knife clattered to the stone floor.

Gilarth leant over the trestle, grabbed Fenna by the collar and lifted him up until his feet left the ground. 'Got any more contraband?'

The thug's face paled to chalk. He squirmed and whined. 'What did we do? Those monsters attacked us.'

'Resisting a lawful search for one,' Gilarth gave the man a shake. 'And not by what I saw. If the Forest Folk wished you harm, you'd be ripped to cotton threads by now.'

Retza picked up the knife, his heartbeat slowing to normal.

A blur caught the corner of his eye, Retza spun round and stuck his leg out, tripping up Darin who was making another run for the door.

Gilarth shook his head. 'Really, Darin? Right, let's get you all roped, and we'll hear your stories in the holding cells.'

The holding cells were directly under the Grand Cavern, accessed through the stairs in the Watcher's ready room. There wasn't a watcher at the door and only one stood guard at the entrance to the holding cells. Two guards lounged outside a cell further down the corridor.

'Here,' Gilarth unlocked a grated gate and untied them one at a time, 'This will do until we sort you out first shift.' He shoved the two bigwuns and Fenna into one cell, and Darin and the other two in another before locking the gates.

Gilarth beckoned, 'Come, Retza.' He took the stairs two at a time and walked to an open area with a couple of stone desks and a rack of open niches. A scattering of copper foils lay on the desk. Gilarth pulled out a box half-full with a clutter of makeshift weapons. 'Throw the knife in here.'

Retza did as instructed. 'Why attack the Forest Folk? Are the troublemakers rebels, sir?'

Gilarth stretched his back, then sat at one of the desks, picked up a stylus and scratched names on a copper foil. 'Just letting off steam, most likely. Though there's still those that believe Putarn had the right of it, or even Uzza. There's enough hidden unrest to pop a bore hole.'

'Then where were the w—' Retza bit his tongue, not sure how much to say in front of the man who'd worked for former Overseer Uzza. Havilah seemed to have a prickly trust for him, but who knew what his real motives were.

'Aye, you're right. Should've had more watchers on. But I cut them a bit of slack.' Gilarth rubbed a big hand over his face. 'You may not have noticed, but two thirds of the fallen used to wear bat-leather. My watchers took the brunt of Putarn and Javot's little rebellion, so I'm shorthanded and what watchers I do have left may have imbibed a bit too much in the wake. I hadn't the heart to stop them.'

It was the longest speech Retza had ever heard from the taciturn man. He squirmed a little. He hadn't noticed how many of the dead were Watchers, but it made sense. 'Not my place to judge, sir.'

'Well you should. If those loud-mouthed louts had provoked these Forest Folk, we'd be in even bigger trouble. It shouldn't have happened on my watch.' Gilarth grabbed a jug from the shelf and poured a clear liquid into a clay beaker.

'Hmmm ...' What could he say? He stifled a yawn and edged to the door. 'If you don't need me, I should get some sleep.'

'Stay a moment.' Gilarth poured the liquid into another cup and handed it to Retza. 'I've had my eye on you for a while now. You and your twin got more courage than sense, sometimes, but I could do with more watchers.'

Retza's chest expanded, his shoulders lifted. Being a Watcher was more than an orphan and a commons-brat could hope for, at least before the old Overseer fled and Havilah began drafting crewless. It was still an honour to be asked, something he'd often dreamed of while scrounging in the commons. An uncomfortable thought niggled like a sharp rock. Delvina was more into rescuing strays than bashing heads. She still agonised over that watcher she'd hit, though he was on the mend and her actions had saved lives.

Gilarth was still talking. 'It would be as a trywun to start with. Think about it, lad. You've proved yourself again and again. I need watchers who are not afraid to act, but aren't so smitten with the power, they let it go to their heads. Let me know if you're interested and I'll speak to Havilah for you.'

'I'll need to talk to Delvina. She may prefer staying a messenger.' Retza took a tentative sip of the drink. And choked. Water, pure and chilled.

'Well, the offer is for you lad. I'm not sure your sister is a watcher at heart.'

Retza's shoulders slumped. 'We do things together. We always have.'

Gilarth slugged down his drink and wiped his mouth. 'Hmm, well, I'd rather have the both of you, than neither. And she has guts, no doubt about that.'

'Thanks. I'll talk to Del.'

Delvina threw the felt blanket to one side and sat up, her head grazing the bunk above. The dying notes of the gong announcing the first shift reverberated about the dorm. There was a reason she needed to be up. She yawned, her jaw cracking, and pushed aside the curtain screening her bunk from the others in the dormitory. Many of the curtains were drawn, no doubt the occupants snuggled deeper under their covers, catching up sleep following last night's feast.

She swung her legs to the floor, grabbed her runner garb from her locker and pulled them on.

Grabbing her boots, she shambled into the messengers' common room. A small group of runners stood by the hob speaking together in low tones, the one called Kailah stirring a huge pot of bubbling soup. The faint aroma of mushrooms reminded Delvina that she was hungry again despite the feast last night.

A few off-duty messengers lounged in the corner, slurping soup, talking, or playing cards or stones, or staring at the walls. Most were offspring of the highwuns and leadwuns. She still felt like an impostor, but she had as much right as any to be here.

Delvina ducked her head and angled to an empty table.

Kailah called out, 'Hey trywun, want some soup?'

The others stopped talking and stared at her.

'Thanks.' Delvina mumbled. She changed direction and took the half-filled bowl offered to her. 'Have you seen Retza?'

Kailah shrugged and went back to talking to her companion.

Finding an empty table in the far corner, Delvina inhaled the fragrant steam before taking a careful sip. She rolled her eyes as last night's conversation surfaced. Of course, Retza wasn't in the common room. He'd still be sleeping after staying back to help out Gilarth and she'd agreed to do his shift for him. By the deep, she was late.

Delvina sculled down the rest of the soup, scalding her mouth. She hopped on one foot as she pulled her boots on, then bolted out the door and along the tunnel towards the council rooms.

The shift flashed past like a train of glimmer trucks given full power. She'd run messages for the Farm Lead Hand Gregan about requirements and requisitions, and returned with the Overseer's instructions. She was sent to the lead hands or scrybes of different cribs and storerooms, collecting and returning inventories and reports on food supplies. She'd ferried instructions to the crews assigned to new work in the Cauldron and returned with further requests, queries and requisitions.

With the last message delivered to Thirdwun Danel supervising the work in the Cauldron, she could finally return to the Messenger Crib. She trudged along the causeway toward the north stairs to the Grand Cavern and the west quarter. Her calves and back ached, and all she could think of was pulling off her boots and collapsing in the common room but not before letting Retza know he owed her one. Maybe they could meet up with Zadeki. She hadn't seen any of the Forest Folk all shift.

Her boot touched the first step when the gong signalling the change of shift sounded.

'Hey, Runner Delvina, you heading to the Overseer?' a big voice boomed out.

She made a face, tempted to keep going. Lead Hand Gregan stepped out of the lift cage, face pinked with emotion or exertion, and strode toward her, one arm full of message cylinders. 'What the woman asks is impossible.'

He beckoned for her and she stepped down slowly. At the bottom of the stairs, he thrust the cluster of message cylinders at her. 'Take this and give them to her, not some low-level scrybe, mind. From your hand to hers!'

'Ah ... I'm—'

But Gregan stomped off before she could protest further. Delvina's shoulders sagged, and she let out her frustration in a long guttural sigh. She juggled the copper tubes, clipping them on her belt while thinking about what the Farm Lead Hand could do with his messages. The errand wouldn't take long at least.

Once again, she trudged up the stairs, clinking and clanging the whole way, and headed toward the makeshift offices past the Grand Cavern.

Two watchers let her into the empty reception room. From the sounds, the lone duty scrybe was rummaging around in the records room. Delvina crossed the room and raised her hand to knock against the battered door to

Havilah's inner office. Her fist hovered as she noted the rise and fall of muted voices.

The Overseer was busy. Surely, Gregan's endless messages could wait until first shift. Or she could put the messages in the Overseer's intake basket.

She lowered her hand. Before she could move, the door swung open and Danel stood in the doorway, his eyes tracking from her fist to her face to the jumble of cylinders jostling on her belt, all with the Farm Lead's tag.

Danel's light brown eyebrows slid up. 'Gregan? Again?'

'He instructed that the Overseer receive them personally, but if she is busy ....' After all, Danel wasn't just some minor scrybe. She peered past him as she recognised the tones of the Forest Folk. So this was where Zadeki had got to.

Danel stood to one side. 'Come in and wait. The meeting is almost finished.'

Caught, she stepped over the threshold into the room, looking for an unobtrusive spot.

The Kinleader was speaking '... please no need to punish them on our account. No harm done.'

'Nevertheless, I must apologise for their disrespect, Kinleader Telsima,' Havilah sat hunched forward in her chair.

Gilarth stood behind her, his face grey with fatigue, his large fingers gripping the stock of his whip. On the other side, Nebam stood, legs astride and hands hooked into his belt. Three Forest Folk faced the Overseer, Zadeki with a graze on his right cheek and his face creased in a rare frown. The other two wore their normal calm, benevolent looks.

'Please, it's forgotten,' the Kinleader said.

'Yet ... you are still determined to leave us?'

Leave? Delvina's heart fluttered in her throat like a trapped moth. 'You can't leave,' she blurted out, then covered her mouth. What would they do without the Forest Folk ... without Zadeki.

Havilah frowned at her and Danel. Zadeki glanced up, then looked away, his mouth in a flat line. Had last night's ruckus affronted her friends?

Korak cast her a sympathetic glance. 'At the moment our presence seems more a hindrance than a help. We will bring food when we can, but for now, you need less mouths to feed.'

Zadeki scuffed his sandals on the stone floor.

Havilah sat back in her chair, tapping her fingers on the armrest. 'I've given thought to your words in the farm caverns, Kinleader. I don't like depending on outsiders,' she looked up, 'No offence meant, but our current stores will only last three rosters, yet it will be another five until we can harvest the potatoes. The algae and mushroom farms will not be enough to sustain us. Would these people of Tamrak provide food at least until the potato harvest?'

A glimmer of a smile touched the Kinleader's lips. 'They might, earth-sister.'

Nebam thrust his head forward. 'Why would outsiders give their food to us? What would they want in return?'

'They have a love for gems and metals, as much or more than the Sea Dragon's followers. These you have in plenty. I'm sure they'll agree to a trade,' Highwun Korak said.

'And is that what you want, too?'

'Nebam,' Havilah sat up straight, her eyes blazing purple fire.

'But, Matu, why do they help us, if not in hope of reward?'

Because they are our friends. Because we need them. Delvina clamped down on the words. First the crewless, now Nebam sought to drive Zadeki and his kin away.

Korak's chuckle sliced through the mounting tension. 'Because we'd get no peace from this youngling otherwise.' He gave his son's shoulder a shake.

'We are all children of the Maker, whether we know it or not.' Telsima added. 'And in memory of my dear baba.' She said in softer tones. For her father had been Darane. 'But if our help is no longer needed or wanted ...'

'We are grateful, Kinleader Telsima. And we would gladly give metal and stones.' Havilah stood. 'Would you speak to these Tamrin on our behalf?'

The Kinleader and Korak exchanged gazes.

'We could, though we don't need pretty rocks to weigh us down.' Telsima tapped her lips. 'You should send your own delegation with us, Havilah, a couple of people you can trust.'

Delvina took a step closer. Who would be the lucky person chosen to go?

'Wouldn't more be needed,' Nebam said. 'How fierce are these people?'

'Much like your people, I would say.' The Kinleader sighed.

'I can fly three or at the most four. If you wish a larger delegation, it will take many days to walk across the mountains,' Korak added.

'And you would bring the supplies back?'

'That may be more difficult given how much you need.'

'There is the old King's road from the Gate to Tamrak's city and on to the coast. Your tunnel, when it's finished, should connect up with it,' Kinleader Telsima added.

Gilarth stirred. 'If we found Uzza, we could gain his seal to disarm the traps and open the Gate.'

Nebam glowered at the big Watcher. 'Searching for the old Overseer, dead or alive, is a fool's game—as futile as searching for a speck of gold in a cavern full of tailings. Maybe you should lean on Zara, see if she knows something.'

'I'm sure she'd tell us, if she did.' Havilah glared at her son and the tall Watcher. 'At this stage we need to focus our resources on the farms and the tunnel operations. Please Kinleader, be assured, we are grateful for your help.' She glanced at the timepiece on the wall and cleared her throat. 'When would you leave Highwun Korak?'

'Let's say two hours after sunrise tomorrow.'

'Are you sure, son of my son?' Kinleader Telsima asked.

'I've slept half the night and most of the day away. Besides, it will be downhill most of the way.'

'So amusing,' Telsima pursed her lips. 'Still, sooner is wise. We'll stay in the Cauldron tonight, if you can send your chosen representatives for the children of Tamrak by dawn, daughter of the mountain.'

Havilah stood and smoothed down her crumpled robes. 'Yes, of course, Kinleader. Gilarth will escort you to the Cauldron to ward against further unfortunate incidents.'

Telsima inclined her head and strode to the door, her dark hair loose and flowing behind her. Korak and Zadeki followed her out.

Gilarth hovered a moment on the threshold. 'I need to speak to you about additional watchers, your Honour.'

'Yes,' Havilah said. 'At first shift though.'

Now was her chance. Delvina unhooked the cylinders and moved to get Havilah's attention. 'Ma'am—.'

Nebam threw up his hands. 'I'll rearrange the shift rosters then, see who we can spare for the tunnel.' He turned and stumbled over Delvina before she could step out of the way. Cylinders cascaded onto the floor. 'Blast it, what do you want, Prentice?'

'Sorry, sir,' Delvina crouched down, grabbing at the shiny tubes.

One rolled along the floor, coming to a stop against Danel's boot. He picked it up and handed it to her.

She gulped. 'I've messages for the Overseer from Lead Hand Gregan.'

'And they couldn't wait until first shift?' Nebam gave a forced smile. 'Give them over then and get about your business.' With a wave of his hand, he stepped around her and continued on his path to the door.

'Put them on my desk over there, thank you Delvina.' Havilah ran a hand over her face. 'I'll look at them later. So Danel, have you thought who should go with you to Tarka, the Quartermaster or his secondwun and ... Barekia perhaps, though I think she's too frail for such a journey.'

'Are you sure I'm the best to send, ma'am? I've never been outside—except supervising the work in the Cauldron. I know nothing of these Tamrak abovegrounders.'

'You are my Speaker, Danel. And none of us have been outside, not since the Gate was closed. Except two—' Havilah stopped and gave Delvina a measured look. 'What do you think, Runner Delvina?'

Delvina's heart hopped like a rock-rabbit fleeing the pot. The thought of flying, of seeing the wide world beyond the tunnels she was born in, representing her people ... thrilled and terrified her in equal measure.

'We'll go. I mean I will and Retza too, I'm sure.' Heat rose to her face. 'That is, if you think it a good choice.'

Danel's face brightened. 'That's a grand idea. The Forest Folk respect you.'

Havilah smiled, weariness shedding from her face for a moment. 'And you've flown with them too. All good points. Very well, Messenger Delvina, speak to your brother and be at the Cauldron by sunrise.'

'Yes, your Honour.' She turned to Danel, an irrepressible smile stretching her cheeks. 'Bring something to shade your eyes and layers of cloths and some waterproof wear as outside is unpredictable, burning hot one moment, icy freezing cold the next and stuff like water or snow falls out of the sky.'

Danel smiled at her. 'Thanks, I will.'

'Tomorrow then.' She turned towards the door, in a hurry to find Retza before he left to fill her stint on Second Shift. Perhaps Gregan snagging her just as her shift ended hadn't been such a bad thing after all.

Retza shambled into the shadowed Messenger Crib room, the lights dimmed for the third shift. He hadn't managed to speak to Delvina yet about Gilarth's offer. The thought of joining the Watchers became more appealing by the minute, especially after running to and from the farm caverns and the Cauldron several hours after his shift should have ended. A soft cacophony of heavy breathing and occasional snores came from the curtained-off bunk room. Sleep beckoned, but he needed something to eat and had to find his sister before her shift.

The hob was cold, and the communal pot scraped clean in the food recess. He rummaged around in the lockers for his allotted algae cake and handful of dried mushrooms, a diet which was wearing thin, and ladled drinking water into a clay cup.

Out of habit, he made his way toward the back corner of the eating area. Something or someone in the deep shadows stirred. He started, his cup tilting and sloshing water over his boots.

'Blast it,' he said under his breath. 'Who's there?'

Putting down his food, he grabbed a glimmer torch and aimed it at the shadows. A narrow beam of blue-white light jiggled over Delvina's sleeping face. She clutched the cloak wrapped around her, her head resting against the wall at an odd angle, her face open and vulnerable with deep sleep.

His throat tightened. She must have waited up to talk to him. He'd promised his parents he'd always protect her. He could barely remember them. Just Matu's gentle touch and the strength of Baba's calloused hands. His parents had died heroes in a cave-in. Then, after Da-Baba had died, nobody visited them in the creche. The Commons had been tough, but they had each other. Now they were spending less and less time together. Would it be any different if they both joined the Watchers? He had to tell her of Gilarth's offer, but it could wait. She needed her sleep, they both did.

He stepped backwards, his heel catching on a stool. He hooked a leg around it stopping it from toppling over. His heart beat harder at the near miss. Waking the whole crib would not go down well.

Delvina gave a snort and rubbed her eyes. She sat up straighter, her pale hair sticking out in all directions. 'Retza! 'I need to talk to you.'

'Me too, but, hush, not here.'

'Where then?'

Retza picked up his food and prised a few strands of

algae free as he dismissed options—the Causeway, the Cauldron, the Grand Cavern, their old patch in the Commons.

Delvina smiled. 'I know, what about our secret spot.'

It seemed a lifetime since they'd been there though it was only a few rosters.

'Perfect.' He gulped down the water and bundled up his meagre rations. 'Come on, then,' he whispered.

He headed out of the crib, along the corridor and down the stairs to the Great Causeway, Delvina following. Once there, they walked along counting the paving stones until he found the break in the railings, close to the waterfall.

Retza squeezed through the narrow gap and clambered down the footholds to the hidden ledge only a couple of tanis above the rush of the river. Droplets of spray speckled his face and the roar of water reverberated around him, the memories of their years as crewless flooding him.

'I miss the old days, Del, when it was just you and me against the world.'

Delvina dropped beside him and sat, her back pressed against the slick wall and knees under her chin. 'Yeah, me too. I've some exciting news, though.'

'So have I.' Had Gilarth already spoken to his sister? His heartbeat quickened. Whatever her news was, she was happy about it. Better it come from her. 'Go on, Del.'

Her eyes caught the glimmer of the lights overhead. 'Havilah is sending a delegation to Tamrak's people and she has asked if you and I will go to help advise Danel.'

It was like a shock of cold water on his face. Delegates? Outside? No, never again. He shuddered. The remainder of his algae cake fell from his fingers, glanced off the edge and went twirling down into the raging waters below. He licked dry lips. 'Why us?'

'Because we're the only ones who've been outside, east to the Great Forest. And now we'll go northwest, see an abovegrounder city. It's a mission of great importance and an honour to be asked.' She leant forward, gripping his hands. 'We can help save our people and help Overseer Havilah again. We have to say yes.'

The rumble of the river threatened to drown her words or perhaps it was the roaring in his ears.

'Retza?'

Retza rubbed at the moss and lichen on the wet rock wall. 'But it will be outside with the burning heat of the sun, the biting wind, the endless sky, the weather that changes and ...' ... and the feeling of flying upwards into a vast sky with no ending or edges or boundaries that he understood, no comforting glimmer lights or enclosed solid walls or the relief of being surrounded with his people. Retza's chest tightened ... 'No, I don't think—'

'It won't be like our journey across the mountains. Korak has agreed to fly us there, the whole world laid out beneath us.'

Retza closed his eyes, then opened them. 'That's worse, not better. I near wet myself flying back here. I kept imagining losing grip, of falling. I am never ever getting on a koraktil again. I don't ever want to go further than the Cauldron.'

Delvina's mouth opened into a perfect circle. 'Come on, it was your first time and Korak wouldn't let us fall. It will be exciting. We would be together again, not crossing paths at the turn of the shift if we're lucky.'

She had a point ... but no, no, no. Not this. It was a crazy idea. Besides, if he turned Gilarth down now, would he get another chance to be a watcher? 'Del, they don't need us. The Forest Folk will be there, and Danel will get the hang of it, just like we did. I'm not going outside again. We don't belong out there.'

Delvina's grip on his hand loosened. 'So, we just say no?'

'I've had another offer.'

Delvina looked down. Spray droplets glistened in her hair.

Retza took a deep breath and plunged on. 'After I helped Gilarth take those crewless to the holding cells, he said I'd make a good watcher. How could tunnel-rats like us ever hope to become watchers under the Old Overseer's regime? But you know, I think we could do it.'

'What? But we've always wanted be toolwuns like Baba and Matu.' She brushed spray from her face.

'Things change, right? We're messengers now. Something we could never have imagined. But this, I reckon I'd be good at it. It's like when we lived on the Commons. We didn't go looking for trouble, but we protected our patch. I looked after you, right? Those bullies like Javot and Fenna, soon learned not to mess with us.'

'Yes, but ...'

'It's not about the fighting. If Uzza was still Overseer, I wouldn't consider it. But Havilah is fair and so's Gilarth. They want the best for our people. I would get to protect them from bullies like Putarn.' His face paled. 'That slag heap could have killed you.'

Delvina traced a pattern in the damp rock. 'You would be a good Watcher.'

Retza grinned, he knew Delvina would understand. They'd always been a team. 'But I couldn't be if we went on this crazy trip. We'd have to turn Gilarth down.'

Delvina looked up, her eyes like dark pools in the shadow of the ravine wall. 'Retza, I'm not sure—'

'It's an opportunity to protect our people. That's going to be important in the rosters to come.'

'Maybe. But connecting with the people outside and getting supplies is vital too. The Forest Folk are leaving just after first shift and Havilah will expect us to be there.'

'We've done our bit Delvina and we should stick together. We can leave the dangerous journeys to others. Danel will be fine. Gilarth will put us in the same unit, for sure.'

Delvina looked over his head, towards the water spilling out of the rock wall. 'I guess ... I suppose being a watcher won't be so bad. But ... we'd need to let the Overseer know we won't be taking up her offer.'

'You're a rock, sis.' He knew she'd listen, she always did. He yawned, a sudden weariness stealing over him. 'Can you tell her? I'm heading for my bunk for a few hours' sleep, but maybe start of second shift we can tell Gilarth we're ready to sign up. We'll be together right?'

He barely saw the nod.

'Great.' He pulled her into a tight hug. 'Thanks for understanding, Del. It's going to be okay, you'll see.'

Delvina jogged out from the tunnels into the Cauldron, her eyes heavy with unshed tears and the dregs of troubled sleep. After only a couple of disturbed hours, she'd dragged herself out of her bunk and made a half-hearted attempted to wake Retza. But, despite her efforts, her twin wouldn't stir, and she risked waking the other runners if she continued. Besides, it only needed one of them to tell Havilah neither she nor Retza would go on the mission to Tarka.

It was an honour to be asked and ... and there was no point in wishing for what couldn't be. She'd already told Danel all she knew. She could get used to being a watcher. She and Retza did things together. They were a team, always had been.

Delvina looked up at the tops of the sheer rock walls of the Cauldron glowing golden in early morning. Behind them the tips of the snow-covered peaks jutted into a sky of cobalt blue. The larger moon glowered like a half-closed eye in the west.

Already, the sun sucked the coolness from her skin.

She dodged the smoking tree stumps and newly felled trunks jumbled in the churned-up mud. Around her, toolwuns with wide felt hats hauled fallen trunks and loads of soil to a cluster of makeshift sledges near the entrance, no doubt to be carried below. Still others placed their tools in barrels and headed inside before the sun could blister their skin. In a space of one moonlit night, the small area cleared for the koraktil to land was already four to five times as big.

She gulped in the fresh morning air, heavy with the sharp scents of pine sap, freshly turned soil and wood-smoke. She shouldn't take mind of night dreams fuelled by worry and exhaustion. Nebam and his workwuns would finish the tunnel, Gregan would get the farms going again, Danel and the Forest Folk would bring more food to the caverns, keeping hunger away until the potatoes were ready to harvest.

Light footsteps beat a familiar long-legged rhythm on the churned-up earth behind her and her heart sped in unison. It had to be Zadeki. She turned to face him, her plait swinging and banging into her shoulder.

He loped toward her, dark curls flopping forward into his eyes and a wide grin on his oval face as bright as the silver moon.

'Hey, Delvina, why the sad look?'

'I didn't sleep too well.' Snatches of fast-fading images jumbled together, her people huddled in a tight knot, bones prominent beneath dry, shrivelled skin, the littlewuns wailing with hunger. Inky shadows swirling like giant moths over the glimmer lights, a miasma filling her mouth and nostrils with the scent of despair, seeping into her sinews and bones.

She shivered. Zadeki pulled her into a quick hug, before releasing her.

'Never mind, you can rest on the journey. Overseer Havilah says she's asked you and Retza to come.'

'Yes, but—'

'The Maker be praised, Da-Matu said I could come. My first trip west of the White Mountains.'

Zadeki was going! Delvina felt a stab deep inside. She could be travelling with him. But she'd promised Retza she'd stay. Delvina tried again. 'Oh, but we're not—'

'Where's your pack? Are you travelling as light as my Kin now? Has Retza gone ahead? But come on.' Zadeki set off, though at a slower pace than his previous headlong rush. 'We'll be late. I can't wait to fly the wind currents again. There's nothing better. This is going to be an adventure.' He angled away from the walls to the tall trees in the centre of the Cauldron. 'This way.'

Maybe it was better to save the painful explanations for one telling. Delvina followed her friend, giving a small little hop every few strides to keep up with Zadeki's long legs.

A figure, with broad shoulders and a little taller than the other toolwuns, spoke to the crew boss. Thirdwun Danel. He turned and waved. The sun glinted off his mud-brown hair and his teeth flashed into a grin.

'Wait up, Delvina,' Danel grabbed the pack resting against his legs and jogged towards her and Zadeki. 'Glad you are on time, Runner. You told Retza?'

Delvina opened her mouth and mumbled something vague.

Beyond the edge of the cleared area where arrow-shaped trees, mountain pines as Zadeki called them, marched down the slope to surround the still water of the crescent-shaped tarn in the centre of this over-sized rock-ringed bowl.

'So much wood,' she said to talk about something else. Wood was scarce in the caverns, ever since the Old Overseer's father banned anyone from going outside, even into the Cauldron.

'A veritable treasure trove.' Danel agreed. 'But you would have seen it before, on your journey.' A note of admiration coloured his voice.

'A very fine copse,' Zadeki agreed. 'Though this is nothing compared to the Great Forest.'

Delvina could only agree. There the trees stretched out like the sky with no visible ending. 'So, where is the Overseer?' Surely, they were not the first to arrive.

'On the knoll over there.' Zadeki waved his hand to a small hill by the tarn, gently sloped at one end and with a sharp cliff facing the still waters. 'Baba will need some height to get off the ground.'

They followed Zadeki into the tangled undergrowth beneath the trees. A light breeze soughed through the pine needles and small birds piped a warning in the branches above. A bubble of irritation soured her stomach. Why did Retza find the outside so hard. Sure, it was scary, terrifying even. Her knees shook like a groundquake the first time Korak had flown them into the Cauldron, but her heart thrilled to see the world stretched out below them like an etched map in the Records Room. And now Zadeki was going on this new adventure while she stayed behind.

She dreaded telling him, and Havilah and Danel too. To explain why they weren't going, why she was letting them down. But Retza was her brother.

As the slope grew steeper, the trees became thinner and the undergrowth sparser. At last they emerged into sunlight and took a path to the top of the small knoll.

The Kinleader, Telsima, stood back from the cliff edge, in deep conversation with Havilah, with Gilarth standing arms folded behind them. A pace away, Highwun Korak looked out over the tarn, his white wrap-around-cloth, sarum the Adelphi called it, pulled tight around him. To one side, she recognised the tall, thin women as Telsima's sharp-tongued daughter, Bikan, and on the other, a surly Quartermaster from the storerooms, Narval.

A breeze came out of nowhere, ruffling the water and scattering leaves.

'I guess this is it.' Danel's voice shook, and he gripped his pack tighter.

'You'll be fine, Thirdwun. Just don't look down.' Zadeki thumped Danel between the shoulder blades.

Danel swallowed hard, his eyes showing white, and Delvina covered a smile with her hand, though she could understand his terror.

Telsima's silvery voice floated toward them. 'Korak

Pathfinder, are you ready? Eldest daughter and young Zadeki will accompany you.'

Highwun Korak nodded. 'As you say, Kinleader.'

A long keening call sounded above them and Delvina tipped her head back. The sky was no longer a wall of blue. Clouds, wispy and wet gathered over the head of Mount Pelee and dimmed the searing heat of the sun. A dark dot flew rapidly from the east, taking a winged shape. The keening call came again. Delvina shivered, wondering what it meant.

'Is that trouble?' Danel asked.

Zadeki grinned. 'Looks like Josenif. He and Aunt Bikan arrived last night and the Kinleader asked him to keep an eye on the weather systems rolling in from the Great Forest.'

The eagle swooped down and flew low over their heads. He circled and landed in front of Kinleader Telsima, transforming into Josenif's lanky form.

'Snow storm is coming in from the east, Da-Matu.'

Delvina's heart fluttered. That didn't sound good. Zadeki broke his arm ... or wing ... in a storm that had blanketed the Cauldron knee deep in snow. If the mission was called off, maybe she'd have more time to persuade Retza to come. But then, maybe not. She hadn't realised the journey had shaken him so much.

'Is that a problem? This storm?' Havilah asked.

The Kinleader peered at the mounting clouds. 'Could be. Koraktils especially rely on thermals to fly.'

'Aye, Da-Matu, or strong winds. It could also speed us on our journey, if we stay ahead of it. And if it gets too strong, we find shelter and let it blow over. A storm like that could last days. But we should leave at once, if we're going now.'

Highwun Bikan nodded. 'As we are all here, let's go.'

'Retza isn't here yet,' Danel said.

All eyes turned to Delvina. She cleared a throat suddenly dry. 'He ... he decided not to come, to take up Gilarth's offer of Watcher and ...' and I'm not coming either, the words played out in her head, but she couldn't say them.

Havilah nodded, a look of disappointment in her mauve eyes. 'Gilarth did speak of this. But at least you're coming.'

A flurry of wind rattled the branches of the pine trees and brought the wet scent of snow.

'Three of you will be easier to carry,' Korak said. 'Grab your packs. We need to go.'

He leaned forward, his body enlarging and lengthening, his face forming into a long snout, legs and arms into clawed feet, chest barrelling, wings sprouting from his shoulder blades and a long whip-like tail stretching out behind him, black fur and feathers mingling. He lifted his head and bugled before crouching down, pale belly crushing the aromatic bushes and scraggly grass beneath him. Danel and Delvina fastened on the leather saddle.

'Mount up,' Korak urged, his voice echoing off the cliffside and sending a flock of mountain pigeons scattering into the sky.

Delvina opened her mouth, but the words 'I'm not going' wouldn't come out. She didn't want to be a Watcher. She was happy as a Runner, wanted to go on this mission to see what was beyond the serrated peaks to the north and west, to live up to Overseer Havilah's trust, to fly with Zadeki and the Forest Folk.

'Runner Delvina. Thirdwun Danel. Quartermaster Narval,' Telsima urged. 'Time to go.'

Danel stood as though carved of rock, his face grey and eyes wide. 'I ... I can't do this.'

Narval stood open-mouthed behind him.

'One of you must go,' Bikan spoke sharply, exasperation brimming in her voice.

'It's easy. I'll show you.' Delvina ran up to the koraktil, clambered up his haunches, and grabbing the rope, she swung herself onto the wide back. She turned and held out a hand. 'Come on Thirdwun. I'll tie you on so you can't fall.'

Zadeki gave him a push from behind. 'You'll be fine.'

Danel gulped and clutched his pack to his chest as though it was his lifeline. With a jerk, he scrambled up. Delvina leant down and grabbed his arm, pulling him. Narval took a shaky step forward while Zadeki assisted him from behind. He threw up a rope and she tied them in. With three of them, it was a bit squashed, but the absence of the panniers gave more room.

'Ready?' Korak growled.

Delvina pulled the last knot tight. 'Ready.'

'Hold on then.'

'Go well,' Havilah shouted, her robe flapping in the strengthening wind.

'May the Maker bless your going and coming.' Telsima added. 'I'll send Josenif and some other pathfinders to scout the King's Road to the Gate. It's some time since it was travelled.'

Korak lurched up on all fours legs and loped along the ridge, claws sparking against rock and sending gravel flying. Danel's hands tightened around Delvina's waist, his breath loud in her ear. Narval moaned. She felt the powerful muscles bunch and release beneath them.

Korak picked up speed, a sudden lurch, and he leapt off the edge of the small cliff. Wings thrust down in a powerful beat, angling up and powering down again.

Delvina felt the drumbeat of the koraktil's two hearts, and the in-and-out bellows of his lungs beneath her knees.

The lake rushed toward them, marbled with blue and misty grey and fringed with the shattered reflections of the trees.

'I can't swim,' Danel whispered.

Neither could she. Delvina's heart plummeted.

'We are going to die,' Narval moaned.

The water ruffled beneath the koraktil's mighty wings and spray hit her cheek as a wing tip skimmed across the water.

Another mighty downbeat of black feathered wings, and they seemed to hover for an endless heartbeat, before lifting into the air, angling toward the cliff face of the Cauldron.

Delvina breathed again, her lungs burning for air and tears streaming down her face.

'Woohoo!' She shouted, energy coursing through her, all senses thrumming.

'I feel sick,' Narval mumbled from behind her.

Korak rumbled a laugh. 'Aim well, earthbiter, and hold on. The passage might be rough for a bit. No time for gentle flying.' He spiralled up into the depths of the sky. Two dark-eyed crested eagles weaved around them and each other, one with a streak of grey.

The figures on the ridge dwindled, the higher Korak rose on the drafts of air. They climbed above the rim of the Cauldron, the ranks of snow-capped mountains stretched out below them. To the east, the clouds towered into the sky, coalescing into a green-tinged wall.

'This is going to be fun,' one of the eagles keened close by in Zadeki's cheerful eagle-voice.

Delvina grinned back, her face and hair whipped by

the cold wind. She didn't have a cloak or a pack, but she didn't care. She was with Zadeki on another adventure. The only splinter in her joy, she was leaving without her twin at her side.

But it would only be a few days, a roster at most. Retza would understand .... And when she got back, she'd join the Watchers, if he still thought it so important.

Full-strength glimmer lights seeped through the door into Retza's eyes. Other runners were stirring in the dorms, getting ready for first shift. He rolled over in the narrow bunk and burrowed under the blanket, hoping for a few more moments of sleep. The events of last night nipped and nagged at him. Delvina got some funny ideas sometimes, like setting her heart on flying across the mountains to some aboveground city. The trip to the Forest Folk was terrifying enough and if he had to do it again, he'd rather keep his boots on solid ground. He felt like he'd escaped a cave-in. More times than not, she was right, but not this time.

'Hey, lazy bones, you going to sleep the shift away.'

He sat up with a jerk and clipped his head on the bunk above him. Runner Kailah grinned at him before disappearing through the doorway. Most of the bunks were empty. Blast it, he must have dozed off again. He squinted at the ancient timepiece on the end wall. If he hurried, he and Del should be in time to speak to Gilarth before the start of the second shift.

After a quick visit to the ablutions room, Retza sauntered out into the common room. Kailah stood over the hob, stirring the bubbling pot of yet more mushroom gruel. Delvina wasn't back yet. A strange feeling squirmed inside Retza. Hunger, most likely. He grabbed an algae cake and took the bowl of steaming soup. The Remembering Feast seemed an age away.

'Thanks.'

'Are you looking for your sister?'

'Yeah.' Retza moistened the dried algae with the soup.

'She left with the shapeshifters at the beginning of first shift.'

His mouth full, he nodded and raised his hand. The confusion was understandable, but no need to correct the other runner. Delvina had gone to the Cauldron to say they weren't going.

Kailah twisted her long citrine hair, before lifting a shoulder. 'I'm running for Gregan this shift.' She grimaced.

'Uggh. Good luck,' he commiserated. 'I best get going too.' He slurped down the dregs and followed Kailah out the door, but instead of heading for the stairs to the lifts, took the east passage towards the Watcher quarters.

Gilarth stood by the door, talking to his Secondwun Timon. He looked up as Retza approached, his face lightening. 'Ah, Runner Retza, I half-expected you'd accept the Overseers' mission like your sister. I can understand. It's a great opportunity.'

'What, oh, no. I'm reporting for duty, sir. I'm sure Delvina will join us later.' He glanced over his shoulder, expecting her to come rushing in at any moment.

Gilarth's iron-grey eyes widened and he rubbed his square beard. 'You don't know?'

Retza's stomach twisted in earnest, despite the ball of algae lodged in his stomach. Had the Overseer taken their refusal badly? 'Overseer Havilah did give us the choice.'

'That she did.' Gilarth studied Retza. 'I'm surprised though that you two decided to separate.'

Retza blinked. 'No but ...' What was the man talking about? Separate. Perhaps, Delvina decided to stay on as a messenger. He'd ask her after he finished his shift. 'So ...'

'Which is between the two of you, of course. Korak seemed confident that it's only a day or two to these Tamrin, so they should be back soon enough.' Gilarth slapped him on the shoulder. 'I'm glad you accepted my offer, Prentice. And I must say, I'm not sure if Havilah would have been too happy if both of you had refused to go. Nebam has already accused me of trying to steal his toolwuns. Despite our losses, the Secondwun expects me to keep order, watch the prisoners and protect the Overseer, but he questions every recruit I make. As you know, I'm shorthanded and I can use some good recruits. But first you need some training.'

'Training.' Back to being a trywun. And, had he heard right? Delvina had gone with Korak, and no doubt her new best friend, Zadeki.

'So, you can handle yourself in a fight. If you prove yourself, lad, I'll see you advanced, but better to follow protocol. Manoah will give you your new gear, then report to the duty Trainer.'

How could she leave without a word though?

Gilarth raised his eyebrows and his voice. 'Did you hear me recruit?'

Retza snapped to attention. 'Yes, sir.'

'Dismissed, trywun.'

Retza headed toward the requisitions and training halls. He tried to pull himself together. It was only a few days and it wasn't as if he couldn't do stuff without his twin. They weren't littlewuns clinging together in the creche anymore.

But she'd gone without him into unknown dangers, when she'd agreed to stay.

Something tilted inside him, hardening like freshly poured slurry. For the first time in his life, he was on his own. Just like his parents and his grandfather, his sister had left him.

Zadeki's muscles ached. He loved flying, but today had been difficult, buffeted by air pockets and sudden downdrafts that barely troubled Baba in his koraktil form. Besides, the snowstorm closing in on their tail feathers unsettled him. The last one he'd encountered had thrown him about like a dried leaf and snapped him like a twig.

The koraktil glided on the air currents with an occasional powerful flap. The mountain eagle form could fly faster for shorter distances, but nothing matched the power and endurance of the fire-beast. It was a form difficult to learn, harder to master, but he was determined one day he would. He blinked. A mob of fat wallaru hopped through the scrub on the mountainside far below him.

'The koraktil will need to keep altitude.' Aunt Bikan's voice sounded in his ear. 'Eat on the wing, if you're hungry.'

He didn't bother to reply. He knew that. He was hungry, but he wasn't so inexperienced that he'd allow his eagle instincts to take over.

He tilted, flight feathers testing the air currents, avoiding downdrafts as much as he could.

The three Darane sat huddled on Baba's broad back. Narval's face rigid, his arms clinging to Danel in front. Danel, his eyes squeezed tightly shut. Delvina with eyes wide with interest, the tip of her snub nose bluish and, despite Baba's heat, her chin quivering. Icicles clung to their hair and Danel's short beard.

Behind them, in the south-east, the clouds boiled and coalesced, cloaking the mountain peaks from full view. In between the peaks stretches of plateau were covered in stumpy cacti and clumps of spiky grass. Ahead, the sun sank towards the long purple line of snow-capped mountains.

'How much further?' he projected his voice into the wind, towards his aunt. 'Will we stop for the evening?'

'By the Maker's favour, the storm winds have carried us further along, and since I've got the height, I'd like to keep going,' Baba replied.

Aunt Bikan dipped her wings. 'As you wish, Korak Pathfinder.'

They flew on in silence, just the whistle of the air slipping past, the crumpled ground speeding beneath them, blue shadows stretching out from the west, swallowing mountain and plain alike. The molten gold of the sun's disc slipped below the chevroned edge of the mountain range, a soft golden-pink blushing the sky. They flew over a large lake, then a series of jagged peaks. A cold wind fanned Zadeki's crest and he pulled his wings down in a powerful stroke to maintain momentum.

'Almost there,' Baba huffed. 'Tarka is just beyond the ridge.'

Some of the mountain slopes were terraced, and clusters of adobe huts perched on sharp ridges. A round golden basin bisected by the pink-gold ribbon of water appeared beyond the ridge. Dwellings covered the slope above the valley, and hovering above them like two sentinels, snow-covered peaks, one larger than the other.

Takra and the twin peaks. It had to be. 'We're here,' Zadeki keened to Delvina and Danel.

Delvina grinned and Danel nodded weakly, one hand

pressed against his mouth. The Quartermaster gave a tight nod, his fingers clutching Baba's fur.

'Indeed. But let's rest with our Kin tonight,' Bikan keened. 'It's not much further.'

Baba nodded and veered west, over another sharp ridge and angled down into a small hidden valley. The river roared over the cliff edge at the head of the ravine into a turbulent pool, overflowing into churning stream below. Strands of red-gold lights winked between the shadowy mass of the night-filled trees. Baba dropped like a stone skittering off the edge of a mountain, pulling up and landing on a small glade beside the river.

Zadeki followed close behind, changing shape as the ground rushed to meet him. He felt loamy soil under his feet, and stretching out his arms sideways, slowed to a stop, his muscles buzzing with the thrill of flight. Aunt Bikan landed elegantly beside him.

Delvina was shivering and her hands were slipping on the frozen knots. Zadeki helped her unfasten them and together, they untied Danel and Narval and helped them down.

The Quartermaster fell on his knees and pulled up handfuls of the grass and laughed hysterically. 'By the powers that be, we survived.'

'Did you doubt it?' Baba boomed.

'I thought I saw structures in the other valley? Why did we land here?' Delvina asked, rubbing her hands together and blowing on her blue-tinged fingers.

'We'll rest here tonight, mountain's daughter, and visit the Kapok on the morrow.'

'Koraktil, koraktil!' A merry shout went up.

The glade was suddenly full of children, laughing and throwing greetings at them, their elders crowding behind. Curiosity hung heavy, like the smell of rain on a humid afternoon. Zadeki felt a grin bubbling up. He may not be in the Great Forest, but he was among his Kin once again and it felt good.

'Sister.' A man with a sprinkling of white in his ruby-red hair, strode through the trees and into the glade. His emerald-green eyes glowed in the gloaming and his face split into a grin. He hugged Aunt Bikan lifting her off her feet. Zadeki's eyes nearly popped at the familiarly.

Baba reared up and his koraktil form melted into his familiar form, exhaustion visible like a heavy cloak dragging him down.

The man turned and embraced him. 'Korak, son of my heart, it's been too long since I've seen you.'

'So it has, Baba. You do remember, Jazadek, though he was a youngling the last time you visited the Forest? Zadeki, come and greet, your da-baba.'

Zadeki responded to his da-baba's infectious smile. Jasalim and Bikan were brother and sister, yet they could not be more different. One severe and thorough, the other merry and welcoming. Though, at this moment, Aunt Bikan was wreathed in smiles.

'Ah, he is as tall as you now and has your look. And who are these others you bring?'

'They seek an audience with the Kapok and to ask if they would give food to Darian's children.'

Da-baba grew still. 'The first we can achieve tomorrow. The second may be far more difficult. Come now, rest and eat.'

He beckoned them to follow him to another clearing. In the centre, red-gold sparks from a roaring fire wound upwards into the velvet darkness, like promises, tokens of bright hopes.

Delvina sat bolt upright. The mat beneath her seemed to sway, no doubt a result of the long hours of flying astride the koraktil yesterday. She looked around wildly. The small room was empty. Curved wood walls gleamed in the honeyed light streaming through an arched window. Her boots and folded jerkin sat at the foot of the sleeping mat, and beside them, a wooden tray with bowls filled with honey comb, berries and small flat cakes and a beaker of clear water. The scent of green leaves, leaf mulch and flowers floated through the open doorway. Outside, a riot of sounds, screeches, trills and the fluting calls of birds and the laughter of children piercing the deep roar of a nearby waterfall.

Were they in Tarka already? She hadn't seen any wooden dwellings last night. The evening was a blur, fleeting images of being offered roasted fish, roots and berries and then falling asleep lulled by the lyrical voices of the Forest Folk under bright stars like glow-worms stranded across the high cavern roof.

She ran fingers through her tangled hair. She needed to freshen up, but first food. She scooped up the honeycomb, tasted liquid light.

Melodic laugher came from the doorway and she snapped her head up. Zadeki stood just outside, his white sarum wrapped around his waist and draped over one shoulder. 'I thought you'd like the honey.'

Delvina licked a sticky finger and made a face at him. 'Where are we?'

'Elder Jasalim's encampment.' Zadeki ducked his head under the arch of the doorway and stepped inside, the floor seeming to sway beneath him. 'You passed out last night. It was a long flight.'

Delvina rocked back on her heels. 'I don't remember.

Then we aren't in Tarka?'

'No. Aunt Bikan is anxious to leave for the Golden Halls. She asked me to check whether you, Danel and Quartermaster Narval still slumber.'

'I thought your people moved across the land, not living in permanent dwellings.'

'True, but some of our meeting places are more permanent, like this one. The first Kinleader is buried here and this settlement aids our dealings with Tamrak's children. Someday I can tell you more of the song of our people.'

'These Tamrak helped you build this village?'

Zadeki tilted his head and grinned. 'No. The Tamrin and the other Filane prefer to build in stone or clay. Come, if you have eaten your fill, I can show you where to wash. Give me a call when you are ready.' He disappeared through the woven cloth covering the doorway.

Delvina washed her face and hands and re-plaited her hair. Once finished, she hopped through the doorway, pulling on her last boot, and froze.

Dense foliage whispered around her on all sides and a plank walkway swayed beneath her feet. Her heart hammered like tongs on metal. With a whimper, she grabbed the rope railing until her knuckles whitened.

No wonder she hadn't seen any dwellings. They were all built high up on the smooth tree trunks, connected by ropes and slatted walkways. Above her the dense foliage of the tree rustled and swayed in the wind. She peered over the side to the ground far below. She was at least three tanis above the ground. Her knees went weak, her limbs turned to slurry and her mouth tasted of cave dust. This was worse than flying.

Zadeki dropped down from the branch above her,

Stone of the Sea

setting her bridge swinging. She grabbed hold of him.

He patted her back. 'Don't worry, Del, the houses and netways are more solid than they look.'

'How did I get up this high?'

'We carried you, daughter of the earth.' Zadeki's dababa, Jasalim, called out from the ground.

'Come on down, it is time to leave.' Highwun Bikan added.

'Are ... Are we flying?'

'No, Korak Pathfinder needs to rest. We will walk unless you wish to ride. Many of us know the horse form.'

Danel emerged from behind the tree. 'No, no. Walking will be fine, I'm sure.'

'How do I get down?' Delvina asked, looking for a glimmer-lift or stairs.

'Well ... a bit far for you to jump and I guess you don't fly.' Zadeki crouched down and pulled out a rope ladder, throwing it over the side. 'Here, let me help you.'

Delvina pushed aside the outstretched hand. She turned, gripped the rope and felt for the first step. She imagined she was descending a mineshaft, with solid metal rungs under her boots and comforting glimmer lights beaming down on her.

She scrambled down and stood a moment until the ground stopped swaying.

Highwun Bikan pulled her flowing tari tighter. 'Let's seek audience with Wulapa Kapok.'

Highwun Jasalim spread out his hands. 'Ah, Wulapa is Kapok no longer, eldest sister.'

'Really? Was it not a few years ago that the young man took over from his father?'

'A couple of ten-years ago now, sister of mine, though

Wulapa's death was unexpected. A hunting accident a few years past. His son is very young.'

'They live such short lives.' Aunt Bikan shook her head. 'Like younglings, all of them, even the grey-heads. Desert flowers that bloom and wither in a day. And this son, what is his character? Will he help our Mountain cousins?'

'He is thoughtful if a little impetuous. His mother handed over the regency at the last New Beginnings Feast, once he completed his Trial of Tears. Still, he has seen just sixteen cycles of the sun's song.'

'More young hot-heads to rush into danger.' Bikan's gaze snagged Zadeki's before grimacing. 'Well, shall we go?'

Danel stepped out from the shadow of a nearby tree, his eyes a little wild. He cleared his throat and adjusted the pack on his shoulder. 'Yes, lead the way, highwuns.'

Bikan took the lead, the others following her along the path winding to the head of the valley beside the white rush of waterfall.

Delvina shot Danel and Narval a sympathetic look. She hoped this boy-Kapok would listen to their pleas and they could soon return home to the caverns with welcome news.

Sweat rolled down Delvina's face and her skin burned under the hot sun. Danel and Narval puffed beside her, faces florid pink. The Forest Folk slowed their long strides or waited every now and then for them to catch up.

On either side of the road, tall plants stood in rows, their dried yellow leaves rustling in the fitful breeze. The only shade was an occasional tree on the side of the road.

The fields stretched out across the valley and in terraces on the surrounding hilly slopes.

'Maize plants,' Zadeki said. 'It's what they eat here.'

Delvina nodded and wiped the sweat from her eyes. People with different shades of light brown skin and colourful clothing worked in the fields, walked along the roads or clustered around the orange-clay houses thatched with straw. Women, with littlewuns tied to their back by swathes of cloth, put down hoes or stopped weaving on wooden looms. Shouting and laughing children with scant clothing and bare feet, strapping young men carrying loads, and white-haired oldwuns crowded behind the delegation as they passed by. Not much taller than Danel, they jabbered away in a confusion of strange sounds.

Delvina's heart skipped when an oldwun reached out and fingered her plait. She flinched, and the crowd tittered. She suddenly longed to be high up above it all, away from prying eyes, blistering sun and dusty road.

'What are they saying, Zadeki?' Danel puffed. 'Do they mean us harm?'

'They are trying to work you out. Some think you might be ghosts, because your skin is like bleached bone and your eyes and hair are so pale. Others that you might be malformed children.'

Quartermaster Narval harrumphed. 'You understand their babble?'

'Since when did children grow beards,' Danel growled. 'Besides you shapeshifters are whiter.'

Zadeki threw a grin at Danel, then turned to Narval. 'Yes, I understand their words, though not as well as Da-Baba. Don't worry though, the Kapok and his advisors speak the ancient tongue. They are just curious and mean you no harm.'

The road left behind seared yellow fields and climbed up a steep hill at the base of the two peaks. Light bounced off the stone road and off the painted mud walls and steep angular roofs of the houses clustered on either side. The open sky pressed down, making it hard to breathe.

'We are almost there. See.' Zadeki pointed up to a large stone house crouching on the first crest of the hill and surrounded by a high red wall. Beyond the hulking building, across a shallow valley, another triangular building and two snow-capped peaks they'd seen the previous day jutted into the sky. The sun had risen halfway up in the sky by the time they'd crested the hill and approached the gates, flanked by two tall towers.

Delvina jumped at the long mournful blasts of a horn coming from one of the towers and the gates swung open.

'The Kapok's palace,' Highwun Bikan said. 'Not quite a cave, but as solid as the stonemasons can make it. Perhaps you will feel more at home here, children of the mountain.'

Danel gazed upwards, his lead-grey eyes alive with interest. 'A sturdy structure indeed, Highwun.'

Delvina could only agree, relieved that these children of Tamrak were not forest dwellers like Zadeki's Kin. Even so, she felt a little intimidated at the scale of the building looming over them like a small hill.

The Forest Folk came to a stop in front of the sweep of marble steps. The dense shade of the building bringing a sudden welcome chill to Delvina's burning skin. At the top, two bronze skinned men clutched what looked like wooden lift-bars topped with bronze blades.

They barked out foreign words and crossed the poles in front of them.

Highwun Jasalim stepped forward. 'We seek an audience with the Kapok.' And then he replied in a string of garbled words.

The bronzed men uncrossed their weapons, banging the wooden ends on the stone steps. '*Hayku.*'

The big doors swung open and moments later a man with a rust-brown cloak and a mass of brown and grey feathers on his head, stepped out. He scanned the group, lingering on Delvina, Danel and Narval, before bringing a closed hand to the centre of his chest and bowing from the waist.

'Wise-one Jasalim, your people are always welcome.' The words were heavily-accented Eldar, but if Delvina concentrated she could understand them.

'Greetings, Madomo Nakrin. On behalf of the people under the mountain, we seek an audience with Supak Kapok, son of Wulapa.'

The man's face remained impassive. 'The Kapok would be honoured to meet with you and your ... friends. *Hayku, kumma.* Come.'

'Our thanks, friend. Lead on.'

Madomo Nakrin walked back into the building and Jasalim beckoned them to follow.

Danel stepped forward, his eyes flitting from the carved stone columns, arches, cornices and other architectural features of the cavernous entrance room. 'Amazing.'

'Yes, yes, but is it secure? Surely it needs more columns.' Narval hovered on the doorstep, his hands clutching his beard.

Madomo Nakrin spun round, his nostrils flaring. 'Of course, it is safe. Come inside, if you please.'

Highwun Bikan sniffed. 'Hush, don't insult our guests.

If it's stood a few centuries, I'm sure it will stand for a few more hours.' She walked forward.

Delvina took a deep breath and followed her. The others filed in behind. The room was as vast as the Grand Cavern and taller. Rectangular patches of light filtered down from lofty skylights.

The Madomo led across the hall, up a flight of stairs and into a long spacious room with narrow windows. A crowd of people dressed in rich tunics, sparkling jewellery and feathered headdresses jostled in front of them. Even the least was dressed as finely and elaborately as the old overseer Uzza.

At first, she thought them all women, as like the Adelphi, none of the men had beards. Then she realised the women had long tunics to their ankles and their dark-brown hair caught up in elaborate arrangements on their heads, while the men wore tunic and breeches and had more prominent noses. The people parted to allow them through, their curious eyes and whispers following their progress. Some hands reached out to touch them.

The last of the people moved to the side to reveal a skinny youngwun lounging on a high-backed golden chair. Inquisitive green eyes flashed in a face the colour of ochre.

Madomo Nakrin lowered himself to the ground and spoke a torrent of words to the boy Kapok, who waved a hand. Nakrin stood up. 'The Adelphi and their pale-skin friends, Your Majesty.'

'Welcome to my halls.' the boy said in a voice not yet settled in its deeper tones, though he was taller than many of those present. He leaned forward, sending the long green and red feathers of his elaborate headdress nodding. Tan fingers stroked the carved jaguar heads on the arms of the chair.

'*Wahayku*. Welcome, Friend Jasalim, it is good to see you again and your Kin. Who have you brought to meet me?'

Highwun Bikan stepped forward, flanked by Jasalim and Korak 'We bring greetings from the Great Forest, child of Tamrak, and from the Kinleader Telsima.'

An older woman, with dangling gold earrings and deep brown hair shot through with grey, stepped forward with a warm smile. Her fingers brushed the Kapok's shoulder. The family resemblance between them was clear.

'Welcome, Friend Jasalim. And welcome Wise Bikan, daughter of Telsima. It is long years since you have graced us with your presence, my Lady.'

Bikan inclined her head. 'I regret to hear of Wulapa Kapok's passing but am glad to see you and your son in good health, Kupanna Adrilla.'

The Kupanna bowed her head, her dark brown eyes welling with sadness. 'Thank you. It is five years since my dear husband's death. One learns to bear it.'

The young Kapok leaned forward. 'Jasalim, please introduce us to your strange friends.' His bright eyes bored into Delvina, then skipped to Danel and Narval. 'Where did you find them?'

'You could say, they found us.' Jasalim waved them closer. 'Havilah, daughter of Elad, Overseer of the Glittering realm under the mountain, sends this delegation to represent her. Thirdwun and Speaker Danel, Quartermaster Narval and Runner Delvina.' Jasalim pointed to each. And then turned to Danel, 'Supak Kapok and his mother, Kupanna Adrilla.'

'Who speaks for these Darane?'

Delvina nudged Danel forward. His voice nub bobbed. 'It is an honour to meet you, Highwun.'

Supak tilted his head. 'Are all your people so pink?'

Kupanna Adrilla placed a hand glittering with gemmed rings, on Supak's arm. 'Supi,' she hissed.

A grimace flashed across the young Kapok's face. He glanced up and sighed. '—but forgive me if I offended.'

Madomo Nakrin pushed forward. 'Perhaps, Your Majesty, your guests would like to refresh. They can speak after the petition time.'

'Nakrin!' Kupanna Adrilla's eyebrows shot up. 'Is this how we treat our Forest friends?'

The Madomo glowered, a vee forming above his hawk-like nose.

The young Kapok wiggled his fingers. 'We are due for a break. Let's retreat to the withdrawing room.' He clapped his hands. 'See to it, my Madomo.'

'As you wish, Your Majesty.' The man left the room, back straight as a ramming pin.

Delvina felt relieved to be free of his scrutiny. She and the others followed the Kapok and Kupanna into a smaller room to the side.

Soon the Madomo returned. Men and women in simpler tunics followed, each carrying trays laden with beakers of drink and platters of strange food, which they offered first to the Kapok and then to Jasalim and Bikan. Others brought chairs.

Delvina took a gulp from a beaker and almost gagged at a sweet liquid, not the water she was expecting, but it slaked her thirst from the long walk to the Palace. She passed on the food.

'I don't think Nakrin likes us much,' Zadeki said in a low voice.

'Will that be a problem?' Danel asked.

Zadeki shrugged.

At the other end of the room, Supak Kapok looked up

from washing his hands. His leaf-green eyes strayed back to Delvina and then to Danel and Narval and he waved them closer to him.

'So, tell us the reason for your visit, Thirdwun Danel.'

Danel took a huge breath. 'Our people live in the mines beneath the mountains to the southeast—'

'Mines, how interesting. To live in the dark tunnels.'

'The Crystal Heart has provided all the light we need to see and grow food up until now.' Danel took a deep breath. 'We ... we have had some difficulties with our farms in recent days.'

Delvina gripped her hands together, examining the closed expression of the Madomo, the warm interest of the Kupanna and the Supak Kapok's eager face. 'We need your help, Highwun.'

Jasalim turned to Supak. 'The mountain people mine the earth, extracting its riches. They would trade such rocks for food and clothing they require.'

'Overseer Havilah thanks you for considering our plight and would be honoured if you accepted this as a gift.'

Danel pulled out a small casket and opened the lid. Precious stones—diamonds, greenstone, rubies—gold chains and other jewellery sparkled in the sunlight splashing through the window. He pulled out a chain of three twisted strands of white, yellow and red gold. A pendant with a large emerald rimmed in diamonds hung from the bottom. He dipped his head and placed it into Madomo Nakrin's outstretched hand, who then handed it to the young Kapok.

Supak lifted the chain. 'I'm sure we could help. Tell us what you need.'

Delvina started breathing again, pleased it was this

easy. It would take time to get the supplies back to the Glittering Realms, but the supplies the Adelphi had brought would give them that.

Danel waved to Delvina. Swallowing, she took the rolled-up foil from the messenger cylinder and offered it to the young Kapok. He waved a hand, and Madomo Nakrin took it, running an eye over the figures inscribed on its shiny surface.

Danel continued. 'Our need for food is desperate. Due to the blight in our potato farms, our supplies are likely to fail and our people to starve within three or more tens-days, many rosters before our reseeded potatoes will yield their harvest. We have more such gems, also refined metals and finely made objects.'

Nakrin waved the foil. 'Food for over four thousand for two Alume. These are not small requests. Have you sent similar requests to Shanti or Silisea?'

'Friend Nakrin, your realm is the closest, your fields the most bountiful.'

'We will do what we can,' Kupanna Adrilla said.

'Your Majesty, Lady Kupanna, of course you should help—' Nakrin gripped his hands together, '—but you will also consider the needs of our own people. We shouldn't be hasty in making promises we might regret.'

Delvina's stomach crawled at something in the Madomo's tone. But it was the Kapok's decision as Overseer of his people.

Supak sat straighter and ran a hand along the curved armrests of his chair. 'My people's needs are indeed my constant concern. We will give this some consideration.'

Bikan clicked her tongue. 'Your fields are plump with maize.'

'It is still two ten-days to harvest,' Nakrin murmured.

'We should not be in haste, for impatience is the seed of error.'

The Kupanna sighed and placed her hand on Supak's shoulder. 'Yet the Maker rewards generosity.'

Supak Kapok looked between his Madomo and his mother, face clamped in an uncertain frown. He ran his fingers along the twisting chain. 'Speaker Danel, my thanks for the Overseer's generous gift. We will help, but Madomo Nakrin raises important considerations that we should think on. In the meantime, please be our guests.'

Danel stood taller. 'As you wish, Your Honour. If you would grace us with a quick decision.'

'Indeed, now my people await. Please make yourselves comfortable here while my Madomo prepares guest rooms for you.' With that he stood and swept out of the room, followed by his entourage, leaving disappointment in his wake.

Delvina turned to the Forest Folk. 'Was that a yes or no?'

Danel shook his head and shrugged. 'A maybe?'

'So it seems.' Bikan clicked her tongue. 'They have plenty of stored food. What is the boy playing at?'

Highwun Jasalim ran a hand through his rust-red curls. 'Power games, I suspect. Give them time to think it through and, by the Maker's favour, they'll give out of their bounty.'

Zadeki touched Delvina's shoulder. 'Don't worry, we will get help for you. If the Kapok won't help, maybe the other Filane will.'

Delvina nodded and stared at the mosaic floor. She hoped that wouldn't be necessary, another journey and more time lost with no greater hope that help would be forthcoming.

Retza pushed the mop over the stone floor of the duty room. When he'd volunteered to be a Watcher he hadn't expected to be doing the drone chores of a trywun again. Despite the desperate need for watchers, Gilarth seemed determined to train his new recruits. That included long hours of running through tunnels, practice fights and picking up after the fully-fledged watchers.

Not that it was that bad really, but doing it without his twin was like walking one-legged. He had a few things to say when she got back about leaving like that. She would be back soon enough. If she wanted to be a runner all her life, that was fine by him, just so long as she worked out this strange desire to leave the tunnels. He grabbed the bucket and took a step backward, barging into the desk. Charts and cylinders went rolling, falling in a crash and clatter to the floor.

Blast it.

Wiping his wet hands on his breeches, he crouched to pick up the mess. One of the charts spooled out into his hands, revealing a carefully drawn map of the levels and areas within the realm. His eyes widened. He never knew there were so many. He flattened it out on the nearby table and traced the tunnels with a calloused finger, twenty-one levels and a scratched out area beneath with strange symbols marking it. And to the north and south other areas.

'Trywun Retza! What are you doing?' Gilarth glared at him from the doorway.

Retza jumped out of his skin like a moulting cave cricket and rolled up the copper foil with fumbling fingers. Double blast it, for a big tall man Gilarth walked like a shadow.

'Er, sorry sir, I knocked them over. Just putting them back,' he mumbled.

Gilarth snorted. 'Yeah, right. You and your sister have a penchant for sticking your snub noses where they aren't supposed to be.'

Retza's scanty meal soured in his gut.

In a couple of strides, Gilarth crossed the room and pulled the chart from Retza's nerveless hands. 'Find anything that interests you?'

'I never knew the realm was so deep. Twenty-one levels ...' Silly, that wasn't a real question. The Head Watcher's voice had dripped with sarcasm.

'Twenty-two levels.' Gilarth rolled the thin foil with practised ease and slipped it back into the cylinder, then grimaced. 'No, you're right ... twenty-one.'

'What are the other areas?' Retza was pushing his luck, but he wanted to know.

'The realm once was three times the size, with three crystal hearts. But one by one the other two failed. We think Uzza—or more likely his corpse by now —is holed up in one of the other areas.'

Excitement thrilled through Retza. 'If we found him and took the seal, we or maybe Zara, could open the gate, making the effort of digging the tunnel unnecessary.'

Gilarth pushed back his bat-leather helmet on his forehead. Deep lines had accumulated around his eyes and mouth. 'Not so easy, though. We collapsed a lot of the tunnels and reinforced walls to prevent the Old Guard attacks. And even without that, it could take years to search them.'

'So Secondwun Nebam's tunnel is our best hope.' If Danel's mission to the Tamrin was successful. But, why wouldn't it be. 'Nothing to worry about. Right?'

'That's about the size of it.' Uncertainty flashed across Gilarth's square face before he smoothed out the worry lines.

Retza's heart fluttered. 'Why is it taking so long though?'

'Have you been to the Gate, Trywun?'

Retza shook his head. 'It was forbidden to approach it under the Old Overseer.'

'That doesn't seem to stop you accessing the Cauldron or top-secret charts either.' Gilarth gave a sudden grin. 'I like your initiative, if not your talent for getting into trouble. The 'gate' is in fact seven complex defensive gates each at least a lek apart.' He stroked his beard. 'And the tunnel between these gates follows a fault in the diorite. It's no easy feat to bypass it.'

'So looking for the seal wouldn't be such a bad idea.'

Gilarth gave a sharp nod. 'But without more watchers assigned to the task, that's not likely to happen. Not without a better idea where to look.'

'Weren't you head of his personal guard? Wouldn't you know?' Retza clamped his mouth shut. Such impertinent talk would attract harsh correction under the Old Overseer.

Gilarth stared at him for a long moment. 'Was. Fact is, I got demoted after ...' Gilarth pushed his lips together. '... a long time ago. Besides, I've already looked in all the places I think the Overseer would have gone to.' He looked thoughtful. 'It's possible that Lady Zara may have some notion where he went, a prepared bolthole perhaps, but I'm not her favourite person any more. Not since I joined up with Havilah.'

Retza shrugged. 'She's Uzza's daughter and doesn't have a high opinion of us lowwuns. Not that you're a lowwun.' Why was Gilarth telling him this. Maybe he just needed someone to bounce ideas off.

Gilarth gave a dismissive wave. 'I might as well have been a drudge to Uzza's family. So, have you any brighter ideas, or are you going to finish cleaning up my Ready Room?'

Retza picked up the mop and suppressed a grimace. If he didn't keep moving, he'd earn Secondwun Timon's ire for not finishing his duties.

Gilarth stepped to the table and tidied up the charts. 'She might tell you.'

Retza fumbled with the mop, lunging after it before it crashed to the floor. 'What? Me?'

'Sure, why not. You're a strapping young fellow about her age. She knows you. Worth a try. I'm assigning you to her watch from tomorrow, Watcher Retza.'

Great, now he was on babysitting-Zara duties. Serve him right for poking his nose in where it wasn't wanted. Then the word clicked. A rush of excitement collided with confusion. Did he say ... 'Watcher, you mean ...'

'I was going to tell you at the end of the shift, but since I found you ...' Gilarth pulled out a bundle of watcher gear from a niche and tossed it to him. 'Finish up here and get ready. We'll have a more formal ceremony for you and the others at third gong tonight.'

Retza dropped the mop handle and caught the items. 'Thank you, sir.'

'No pressure now, but I've a hunch we might need that seal to survive.'

As Retza walked back to the crib room he mulled over his new detail. If the fate of the Glittering Realms depended on his connection with Zara, they were in deep trouble.

Retza pulled at the heavy bat-leather pants as he walked down the tunnel toward the Heart Room with his shift mates, four men he barely knew. The new helmet pressed down on his ears and already his hair itched. Perhaps he should get the shorter haircut most Watchers preferred. Both the truncheon on one side, and the coiled whip on the other, banged against his thighs with every step. To be honest, he'd prefer his lift-bar.

No word from Delvina or the delegation to Tamrak's people as yet. No doubt she was having a fine time riding along on an important mission. Retza gave a tight-lipped smile. If he'd known he'd be stuck with guarding Zara, maybe he would have gone with Del. The Overseer's daughter had softened when they'd fought Putarn, but, from what the other watchers said, she was back to her haughty ways. He wasn't surprised.

The floor seemed to shift beneath his feet and dust drifted down from the rock roof above.

'What was that?' Retza asked.

'Nebam's using firepowder on the tunnel,' one of the watchers, Manoah, grunted.

Made sense given the squeeze on time. Taking a deep breath, Retza squared his shoulders and approached the door to the Heart Room.

The watchers on duty checked the credentials of Retza and the other replacements, before heading back down the tunnel. Manoah and one of the others stationed themselves outside the Heart Room, while the other two stood inside the door. Retza was assigned the grunt duty of making sure Zara and Jesson's needs were provided for.

The large cavern seemed unchanged from when he was last there. Was it only days ago, before the Remembering ceremony? In the centre of the room, the large blue-green crystals cast shimmering patterns of light across the stone floor and along the walls. The oldwun wasn't there, most likely still in her crib room or poring over codices and scrolls in the records room.

Uzza's children sat at a low table. Zara wrote in a small journal with real paper that only a highwun could hope to possess, head bent in concentration her white-gold hair falling loose about her shoulders.

Jesson glanced up from playing with a toy digger. His bored scowl wavered and vanished, and he tugged on his sister's sleeve. 'Look Zara, it's Retza.'

She flicked a look at him, and then returned her attention to her journal, soft lips in a flat line. Retza sighed and folded his arms. Not a good start. What next? Should he start a conversation?

Jesson jumped up and ran over. 'Why are you wearing watcher leather?'

Retza smiled down at the eager face and tussled the youngwun's hair. 'Because I am a watcher now.'

Zara shifted, her hand tightening on her book. A tremor squirmed in his gut. Despite the ready frown and arrogant tilt of her head, she had the fragile beauty of an ornament, hair like spun gold, translucent soft skin and cobalt blue eyes. Not that he wanted to tangle with Uzza's daughter. The whole family was bad news. Gilarth was delusional to think she would notice a lowwun like him or care what he thought or said, but he had to try at least.

He wet his dry lips, took a sharp breath. 'Lady Zara, I have been assigned to you this shift. Is there anything I can get you?'

She shot him a look, fire in eyes as fathomless as the blue of the sky and as scary.

'How does freedom sound,' she said. 'And justice for usurpers.'

'You know I can't do that.'

'Then you are not much good, are you.' She turned her stool, so all he could see was the soft curve of her cheek, her golden eyelashes and the rigidity of her shoulder blades. 'Come Jesson. Time for your lessons.'

'But Zara ...' Jesson whined.

'I said come.' She pushed a slate across the table towards her brother.

The youngwun gave Retza an apologetic smile and scratched runes on its surface.

Retza glared at the rigid back in the shimmering light. This was going to be a long shift. Did she know where her father could be hiding or the location of the seal? Just as well Nebam had recommended work on the new tunnel. They would be in deep trouble if their fate depended on him prising answers from Uzza's proud daughter.

He only hoped Danel and Delvina were having more success.

'**Five days! How much longer** do we have to wait,' Delvina grumbled.

She paced beside the atrium pool reflecting the darkening sky outside. The palace builders used many cunning means to bring the light and air inside but the feeling of not being either inside or out disoriented her. Perhaps Narval had the right idea, staying in the room allotted him.

Danel turned from running his fingers along a load-bearing column with his ever-cheerful smile. 'We're getting somewhere, I think. Highwun Jasalim says they're interested in what metals we can supply.'

'But will it be enough?'

'I'm not sure. I hope so. Highwun Jasalim speaks eloquently on our behalf. We just have to wait.'

Wait, wait, wait. Talk, talk, talk.

Delvina took a deep, shuddering breath. It was all they seemed to do. Time was slipping past them like a fast underground stream.

The sounds of servants bustling about their duties filtered down the corridor. There seemed no lack of food, no sign of want or need, though perhaps it was different in the smaller houses surrounding the palace? Surely, it was not such a hard decision to help them. What if Supak and that insufferable Nakrin kept them waiting until it was too late to find help elsewhere?

Home. How she longed for the coolness of diorite and andesite beneath her hands, the clean, uncluttered lines of the Great Causeway, where people looked you in the eye and did not prod and poke you as though you were a cave cray ready for the pot. She missed the soft blue glow of the glimmer lights and worried about how Havilah and the others were doing. And most of all, she missed Retza's steady presence. She needed to breathe.

'I think I'll take a walk.'

Wrapping the borrowed Tamrin cloak around her, Delvina headed out of the atrium and along the corridor to the Great Hall.

A blast of warm air hit her face like a furnace door swinging open. Already, the candles in tall wooden stands had been lit. The smell of burning tallow, and the spices and rich roasts drifting in from the kitchen, the clatter of feet on stone floors and trays and excited voices, the strangeness of woven tapestries with exotic picture of hunts, and expeditions and courting couples swaying on the walls. All the richness and clutter pressed down on her until her head spun.

Delvina pushed her way to large doors that led

outside. Chill air slapped her face and nibbled her fingers. She tucked her hands under her arms and stood. The sky deepened to dark-purple, a bright star beamed on the western horizon where the dusty-pink afterglow of the sun brushed the distant mountains.

Inside or out, there was nowhere like the caverns.

Danel caught up with her, his ash-grey eyes troubled. 'The waiting is hard, I know. We need to be patient.'

Delvina nodded, her eyes on the path under her boots. She wanted to storm into the Tamrin's deliberations and demand answers.

Soft voices floated on the air from the direction of the small hill enclosed in the palace gardens. The aromatic smells of green things, the tinkle of a fountain and the night calls of birds surrounded them.

A shape loomed out of the shadows. Delvina's heart skidded to a stop before racing away.

'Braving the outside? Here, come join us.' Zadeki's teeth flashed white in the dark, his face and arms like a silvery after-image.

Her muscles unclenched at the cheerful sound of his voice.

He led them through the trees and bushes rich with floral scents, past open spaces and fountains and up marble stairs to a round stone shelter supported by pillars that stood on top of a small hill. Highwuns Bikan, Jasalim and Korak, with a couple of other Forest Folk she didn't recognise, were grouped around a small fire in the open. They shuffled along and made room for her and Danel on the curved stone benches.

'When will they decide?' Delvina demanded, then regretted her tone. The Forest Folk were doing what they could.

Highwun Bikan turned to Jasalim, sitting cross-legged on a nearby rounded rock. 'You know Tamrak's children best. Do they seek a consensus?'

Jasalim shook his head. 'That is our way, not theirs. In the end, it is the son of Wulapa's decision, but as much as he respects my opinion, Nakrin has a strong influence on him. If it were harvest time already, they would be more open to helping. The last two harvests have been poor.'

One thing was clear, the Tamrin did not lack for food. Perhaps, they cared little about a few thousand strangers slowing starving in the tunnels beneath the mountain. Everywhere they turned, there were obstacles, refusals, reasons not to help.

Delvina closed her eyes and then snapped them open. 'What about the Sea Dragon King? Would he be able to help us? You said he desired metals.'

The Forest Folk fell silent, faces suddenly grave. The night sounds stilled, and Argenti, the smaller silver moon, slipped behind a cloud. Had she said the wrong thing?

Highwun Bikan broke the silence. 'Even if he were inclined to be generous, the Lonely Isles are across the ocean and they depend on the Filane to supply many of their needs. Besides, the Sea Dragon King's help always comes at a great price.'

Danel pulled his borrowed cloak tighter. 'Without food, our people will die. What price is greater than that?'

'To lose one's self, one's honour, one's reason for living.'

Highwun Jasalim sat straighter. 'You can have such food as we have. It won't be enough, but it could help for a time.'

'Then what will you eat?' Danel asked.

Jasalim spread his hands, the fire reflected in his dark eyes. 'It's been many cycles of the sun, but we haven't forgotten how to follow the songlines and forage for food if need be.'

'About time, younger brother.' Bikan leant over and poked him in the midriff. 'Your kin-group grow fat and slow sitting in one place for so long.'

'Who are you calling slow?' With a growl, Jasalim leaned forward and whipped a clip from Highwun Bikan's hair, causing it to cascade down her back.

'Hey, give that back.'

'Catch me, eldest sister.' And with that he leapt off the rock, his limbs stretching into jaguar form before his feet hit the ground. He bounded down the hill, tail stretched out behind him.

Highwun Bikan stood a second, her mouth open. Jasalim stopped at the bottom of the hill, looking back with a sharp-fanged grin. Her lips quirked into a smile. She leapt after him, transforming into a sleek jaguar with silver markings. The two chased each other, twisting and turning. They pounced in the shadows, rolling together and jumping over each other in a tumble of limbs and snapping jaws.

Shocked, Delvina jumped up. 'Should we stop them?'

'Are you offering?' Highwun Korak pushed her back down and laughed. 'Come, you know what siblings are like.' He stood up and poked the fire, sending flames and embers flying up into the purple-black sky. None of the other Forest Folk seemed upset.

Delvina shook her head. These two were oldwuns. She and Retza rarely argued, at least until now. Her mood sank like lead in water. Would he be very cross that she'd left? And for what? She'd had such high hopes for this mission.

'Someone's coming,' Zadeki said.

The orange flame of a torch wound through the garden toward them. The Madomo stepped into the firelight only to jump backward when the two jaguars rolled past him. The whites of his eyes flashed in the gloaming.

One of the jaguars transformed back into the tall agile form of Jasalim.

Bikan shifted into human form beside him, smoothing out her white flowing tari. 'Can we help you, son of Karrak?'

Madomo Nakrin humphed. 'Is the Speaker here?'

Danel gave Delvina a glance. Taking a breath, he stepped forward. 'I am here.'

'Speaker Danel, the Kapok will speak with you at sunrise in the east council room.'

Danel bent his head, 'Tell His Majesty, we will be there.'

The Madomo inclined his head, the feather of his headdress nodding. With a flick of his cloak and sideways look at Jasalim and Bikan, he turned back to the palace, the torchbearer following.

'This is a good sign,' Highwun Korak said.

'That it is,' Highwun Jasalim agreed.

Delvina's heart squeezed tight, hooking her breath. Tomorrow, they'd know what Supak Kapok's decision would be.

Retza stood stiff and straight, wishing fervently that he could scratch beneath his bat-leather jacket. In the centre of the room, old Barekia potted about the Crystal Heart, keeping it humming and the Glimmer lights bright.

Zara remained focused on anything but his attempts to engage her in conversation, except to give the occasional peremptory order. All he had to show was aching calves and feet from standing still for hours on end. He'd rather be patrolling the commons or even be mopping out the crib room. Gilarth was crazy if he thought Retza could win Uzza's proud daughter over.

'Watcher Retza,' the oldwun called. 'I need a hand.'

Retza glanced at the two Watchers on the door and hesitated.

'Come on, don't dawdle.'

'Go help the oldwun. We won't be going anywhere.' Lady Zara looked up and gestured in the direction of the guards at the door.

Retza let out a frustrated breath. It wasn't part of his duty-list but why not. He walked over to the faceted stones that powered their realm, the lights, the ventilation shafts, the farms. His stomach twisted at the thought of the blighted farms and hoped that Gregan had managed to restore them.

'What is it, Scrybe Barekia?'

The oldwun looked thinner, her skin almost transparent. 'I need some of your muscle to loosen this here stubborn wheel.'

Retza stared into the mass of brass wheels and cogs and dials. None of it made much sense to him, though Delvina said ... No, he pushed the thought away. She still hadn't returned. No message or apology for leaving without a word after agreeing to join the Watchers with him. You mean you agreed. Batting the words away, he crouched down and gripped the wheel, twisting it. It wouldn't bulge.

'Is the Heart not working?'

'It's fine, youngwun. But the innards haven't been cleaned or calibrated in a long while. And I'd like to be familiar with every nut and bolt. Have you heard any news from your sister?'

'No.' Nor did he want to. Trouble was, he missed her. He'd always been her protector, hadn't he? And now ... who was he kidding? He was babysitting Uzza's brats and no further in fulfilling Gilarth's misplaced trust in him.

The wheel jerked and spun all of a sudden, cracking his knuckles.

'Ow.'

He snatched his hand away and blew on it. A gust of steam jetted from one of the pipes.

'Steady there.' Barekia eased the wheel back and rubbed the joint with an oil-soaked cloth. 'She still cares for you, Prentice, just your paths are different.'

'Yeah, sure. And it's Watcher now. Is that all you need me for?' He shouldn't be so snappy with the oldwun. None of this was her fault.

'Hand me that manual over there. And for another piece of unwelcome advice—.' Barekia smiled, showing the gaps between her teeth. 'Loosen up with the lass over there. She's scared and lonely, is all.'

Stuck up and bossy more like it. Retza scowled as he grabbed the leather-bound book from the shelf and gave it to the Old Scrybe.

'It's the way she was brought up. You'd be surprised how people can change given a little encouragement.' Then louder. 'That's all for now, Watcher.'

Retza snorted. Zara was about as approachable as a cornered cave bat and he hadn't noticed much change. Well maybe a little. He blinked back the sudden memory of Delvina coaxing and soothing a baby cave bat, avoiding the needle-sharp teeth, wing hooks and claws as she cradled it in her capable hands. Giving him all the reasons why they should return it to its mother rather than add it to the pot and thus fill their empty bellies. He closed his eyes. Zadeki better look after his twin. Her tender heart could get her into all sorts of trouble. But maybe the Scrybe had a point.

He returned to his post. Zara had her head down, eyes fixed on the same page she'd been reading this last hour. Her shoulders were hunched, her back was as tight as a rusty dial. It would be hard to be alone and friendless. As if sensing his thoughts, she shivered. Maybe he could try it Barekia's ... and Delvina's ... way.

'Is there anything you need, Lady Zara?' he asked with a gentler voice.

She darted a glance at him. 'No, and if you don't mind, I'm reading.'

He took a step and staggered when the ground bucked beneath his feet. Furniture rattled, and the Heart Crystals chimed with discordant sounds. He grabbed the table as he fell.

'What was that?'

A series of muffled booms, like distant thunder in the forest, shook the room—stronger this time. Bowls and books crashed to the floor and Jesson screamed. The shaking slowly subsided.

One of the watchers at the door ran to help Barekia up. Zara cradled Jesson protectively on the floor.

Retza brushed himself off and offered an arm to Zara. She hesitated only a moment before gripping his elbow and allowing him to pull her to her feet. She pulled Jesson to her and looked him over, ignoring the graze on her own elbow.

'Are you alright?' she asked.

Jesson nodded, his eyes wide and his face grey with shock. 'What was that?'

Retza shook his head, at a loss for answers. He grabbed the up-turned table and set it back in its spot. Then picked up the broken slate and moved Zara's journal away from the spilled ink seeping across the rug. Dust drifted down from the pipes running along the ceiling from the Crystal Heart.

'Felt like a groundquake or a tunnel collapse,' Barekia gasped. She seemed shaken, but not seriously hurt.

Yes, but why?

Retza's throat tightened. He was just a littlewun when the last groundquakes hit, too young to really remember them, though his parents had died in a cave-in caused by the aftershocks the following year. How big had the collapse been. How much damage had it done? Silence filled the room.

Another shudder ran through the floor, much smaller and only seconds long this time.

The alarm gong sounded. Da-rang, da-rang, da-rang.

Retza rubbed his hands on his breeches. 'I'll find out what's happening.'

Before he reached the door, it swung open and Manoah stepped through.

He gave Retza a curt nod. 'Come with me, Retza. The rest of you stay here and keep to the centre of the room.'

'Shouldn't we all go?' Zara jammed her fists on her hips. Jesson's lower lip trembled.

Manoah scowled. 'Do as you're told, Lady.'

'Until we know what's going on, it's safer here, Lady Zara,' Retza said. He met her sapphire-cold stare but didn't back down.

Barekia nodded. 'Could be more aftershocks. Here we have supplies, water, power and less chance of falling rocks.'

Zara's fair brow crinkled in thought. 'As you wish.'

'Come on, Watcher,' Manoah growled.

Retza turned to follow the taciturn watcher out the door.

'Come back soon,' Zara's soft whisper followed him down the tunnel. 'Be safe.'

'The Kapok is ready to see you now.'

Delvina swallowed against the sudden tightness in her throat and followed Danel and the others into the audience room. She had hardly slept last night, suspended in agony between doubt and hope.

The Supak Kapok sat in a golden high-backed chair at the other end of the room, arrayed in full regalia. He dispensed with the usual formalities. 'Mountain dwellers, we have deliberated and are sympathetic to your plight.' He glanced at his mother, the Kupanna and then to his Madomo, and lifted his chin. 'We will provide the food supplies you require—'

A great weight slipped from Delvina's shoulders and she stifled a relieved cry.

'—though we think it prudent to wait until the maize harvest is brought in.'

What? More waiting. The heaviness slammed back down again. Would it be too late?

Danel voiced her question. 'When is the harvest?'

'A ten-day away at most.' Highwun Jasalim frowned. 'You still have food in your stores, son of Wulapa.'

'Yes, wise-one Jasalim. But until we are sure our harvest is adequate, we will not know how much food we can spare.'

'The maize ears grow plump and plentiful. Your fields full of bounty.' Highwun Bikan's voice was tart, as tart as Delvina felt.

Jasalim placed his hand on his sister's shoulder. 'We appreciate your offer, son of Wulapa. Yet, it would help greatly, if you could spare a portion now to give our mountain friends some breathing room.'

Madomo Nakrin's hand tightened on the back of the Kapok's chair. 'We cannot risk giving away our stores when an untimely frost or snowstorm could change things overnight ...'

Highwun Bikan held out her slender hands. 'Son of Wulapa, not all seasons are bountiful, this is true, yet the Maker rewards those who trust him. Surely, your generosity would be rewarded or your cousins to the north or south could repair your lack, if need be.'

Young Supak squirmed in his big chair. A quick glance at Nakrin and he straightened his back. 'It is but a short time. I will not be moved on this.'

A frown flitted over the Kupanna's face before being replaced by a smile. 'We can provide pack yarmas to transport the food and you are welcome to remain as our guests.'

'Yes, yes, this we can do,' Supak agreed.

Danel turned to the Forest Folk. 'How long would it take to transport the food? Should we seek elsewhere.'

Jasalim ran a hand through his dark hair. 'A couple of ten-days by yarma train.'

'And by koraktil? Korak?'

'Two days flight there and back, but with the number of trips required, even fully loaded it would take us as long, perhaps longer to fly all the stores needed.'

'It would still work.' Quartermaster Narval fiddled with

his belt. 'Our supplies should last two to three ten-days.'

Delvina did the math. 'If the tunnel or Gate is open by then.' Bringing it in by the Cauldron would be a different matter. But it was something at least, a candlelight at the end of a long tunnel.

'Is this agreeable to you, Speaker Danel?' Madomo Nakrin asked.

Danel tugged his beard. 'As Highwun Jasalim says, it leaves no room for the untoward, yet we do appreciate your offer, your Majesty.'

Supak Kapok stood and folded his arms, 'Then we are agreed. Madomo Nakrin will make the arrangements. Please, join us in the Banqueting Hall tonight to celebrate the pact between us.'

'Your Majesty.' Danel bowed and beckoned to Delvina and the others to follow him.

They filed down the stairs, crossed the Great Hall and entered the smaller guest quarters without speaking. The central atrium pool reflected the golden crescent of Alumi swimming in an opal-blue sky. Birdsong drifted in from outside.

Highwun Bikan sighed. 'I'm sure they have food to spare in these stone storerooms. Is there no way, Jasalim, to encourage them to be less cautious and more generous?'

'I fear Madomo Nakrin is using his influence on the young Kapok.'

'Perhaps you could growl at them or threaten to swallow them whole in that giant beast form.' Delvina was only half-joking. She appreciated that the Forest Folk didn't use force to impose their will on others but knowing there was food that could be sent now was frustrating.

'Not such a bad idea,' Quartermaster Narval rocked back on his boots.

Highwun Jasalim raised his red eyebrows. 'And if we did, they might withdraw what support they've already agreed to offer. The Maker's gifts are not to be lightly used.'

'Then, let's hope young Nebam is successful in his tunnelling.' Narval tugged his long-plaited beard.

Danel slapped him on the shoulder. 'The timing is tight, but all going well, the food will arrive in time for our people,'

He was right too. Delvina grinned and clapped her hands. 'Then we did it then. Thank you.'

'Yes, our thanks for your help, Highwuns. Overseer Havilah will be overjoyed at your news.

Bikan tented her hands and bowed. 'The Maker be praised. Celebrations are in order. On the morrow, Zadeki and I fly to the Kinleader and Overseer Havilah to inform them of the situation.'

Delvina only wished she could be there too, to see Retza's reaction at the success of the mission.

Retza and Manoah jogged along the deserted tunnels, skirting small piles of debris. Da-rang, da-rang, da-rang. The alarm echoed off the stone tunnel walls and vibrated in time with his heartbeat.

They reached the Grand Cavern. Oldwuns, carewuns, and littlewuns streamed into the Grand Cavern, eyes wide and uncertain.

'What happened?' Retza asked a greybeard.

Mute, the man shook his head and kept walking.

'Tunnel collapse,' a carewun, herding a group of littlewuns, said.

'If it isn't the Old Guard attacking,' another mumbled, face grey.

Manoah turned to Retza. 'This lot don't know. Let's head to the Watcher duty room,'

They pushed their way through the growing crowd. More shuffled along the concourse outside. Rubble piled against a partially collapsed western entrance to the Overseers' new offices and the messenger cribs.

'Perhaps we should go that way,' Retza said. 'That's where the damage seems worst.'

The other watcher hesitated. 'I don't know, the duty room is the other way.'

'Manoah! Retza! What the blazes are you doing here?'

Retza spun around. Gilarth's tall figure was clearly visible above the heads of crowd. Overseer Havilah walked beside him, a strand of hair loose and dust on her face. She headed toward the Grand Cavern.

'Well?' Gilarth asked, brows crunching together.

'We're finding out what's going on,' Manoah answered.

'Are Lady Zara and Jesson alright?' Gilarth strode toward them, the crowd parting to let him through. Secondwun Timon followed a step behind.

'Yes, they are and old Barekia. Where is the damage? Is the Overseer alright?'

Gilarth nodded, face grim. 'Only minor damage here. The collapse is two levels down.'

Two levels down. Retza's breath caught in a suddenly airless room. The same level as Nebam's tunnel to the outside. The only level with active excavation since Putarn's rebellion.

'... We are directing oldwuns and youngwuns to the Grand Cavern.' Gilarth rubbed his face. 'Okay, Timon, get Lady Zara and Highwun Jesson to a secure place. Leave Scrybe Barekia in Overseer Havilah's care in the Grand Cavern. Then help Overseer Havilah calm the people in the Grand Cavern. Retza and Manoah, come with me.'

Gilarth strode away and took the inner stairs down two at a time. Retza and Manoah hurried to catch up with his long stride.

At the bottom of the first flight down, Kailah and two other runners stood in a huddle, looking lost.

Gilarth beckoned them over. 'Spread the word. Direct oldwuns and youngwuns to the Grand Cavern. All available crews to the staging post to the new tunnel.'

'Yes, sir,' Kailah saluted and she and her companions hurried away.

The air thickened as they approached the staging post. Dust motes spun in the glimmerlight and clogged Retza's nose. Small spider cracks marred some of the support columns.

Gilarth made a straight line to where Nebam stood at the entrance to the western tunnel, his pale ginger head bowed. Toolwuns milled about a line of connected glimmer trucks.

'Form up in an orderly fashion, you slugs,' Izan, the Lead Hand of Copper East bellowed, frustration inscribed all over her face.

'Watch out,' someone shouted, and toolwuns scattered off the rails as a single flatbed glimmer truck emerged from the tunnel.

The front toolwun jumped off and ran up to Secondwun Nebam. 'Full tunnel collapse five lek in, sir. The supports this side seem to be holding and we've cleared the access tracks as far as we can.'

Five lek! Retza stopped mid step, his chest tight. The cave-in must be massive. Which unfortunate crew had been on duty?

'That close?' Nebam gripped the man's arm. 'Any survivors?'

'Not that we can see, sir. No bodies, either.'

Retza's fists tightened. Buried, no doubt, under all that rubble.

Nebam gave a small moan and his bearded chin sunk lower on his chest.

'Did you see evidence of the Old Guard?' Gilarth asked.

'No, sir.'

'That's the least of our worries, Watcher Gilarth. After almost six rosters, not one of Uzza's crew are likely to be alive.' Nebam turned his back and waved at Lead Hand Izan. 'Get this sorry show going. Now!'

Toolwuns carrying pickaxes and shovels shuffled forward. Nebam stepped toward the lead truck.

Gilarth caught his shoulder, 'Sir, you can direct operations from here.'

Nebam shrugged Gilarth's hand off. 'Let go of me. I'll direct from where I see fit.'

'At least let these two come with you.'

Nebam glared. 'If your watchers must come, they better get their backsides on the trucks now.' He strode away.

Manoah gave a half-salute and followed.

As Retza stepped past, Gilarth gripped his shoulder. 'Keep an eye on the Secondwun, he's distraught. And ... if you see anything strange, let me know.'

Retza narrowed eyes. 'Strange, sir? How so?'

'You'll know if you see it,' Gilarth said. The glimmer trucks lurched forward. 'Go on now.'

'Right, sir.' Retza ran to the front and scrambled onto the lead truck behind Nebam and Manoah.

The glimmer trucks picked up speed and hurtled along to the click clack, click clack, click clack beat. Despite the signs of recent activity, this part of the old tunnel still had an abandoned feel. Long festoons of cobwebs hung from the sooty ceiling and a stale musty smell caught in Retza's throat. No one spoke.

After several lek, a large carved gateway loomed ahead of them, two sculpted figures on either side.

'The First Gate.' Manoah whispered.

With a jerk, the lead truck veered to the right, into a smaller tunnel and one less well lit. After a while, large branching cracks ran across the walls and, in places, piles of stone and dirt lay in heaps. The roof was much lower here and glimmer lights had been strung from new beams and temporary struts. The downward slope increased, and the air grew heavier with rock-dust.

Retza swallowed against the tightness in his throat. There was a possibility that these sections could come tumbling down on top of them.

Up ahead the line of glimmer lights disappeared. The trucks slowed to a jogging pace then they squealed to a stop.

'Out. Out. Out,' Lead Hand Izan called.

Retza vaulted out of the truck and joined Nebam. The Secondwun stood at the front, shining his glimmer torch at a jumbled mass of broken rock and earth reaching the tunnel roof.

'Will I get the crew working clearing the rubble, Secondwun?' The Copper East's Lead Hand asked.

Nebam held up a hand, his face ghostly in the flash of the glimmer torch. 'Wait, we should test for stability. Do we have someone who can sing the rocks?'

'Yes, sir. Peta.' Lead Hand Izan beckoned for her stone singer to join her.

'Good. Listen for survivors.'

The Lead Hand nodded. Together she and Peta picked their way over the heap of debris, testing and prodding with lift-bars.

Retza gripped the comforting handle of his truncheon, his eyes straining against the inky blackness. It looked a substantial fall. 'Which crew was on duty?'

'Greenstone South,' Nebam said through tight lips. 'I had just left them.'

Retza's skin crawled. No! Their old crew. The toolwuns' faces flashed before him and his eyes watered. It would be a miracle if any survived.

'The collapse must be big to have felt it all the way to the Heart Room,' Manoah said.

'The tunnel seems stable.' Stone Singer Peta called back, her voice echoing off the walls.

Nebam divided the toolwuns into teams of six to remove the rubble, stopping every so often to listen to possible indications of survivors. They loaded the broken rock and fragmented struts into the glimmer tucks and sent them back down the tunnel. After a time, the trucks returned with new struts and equipment.

The hours ground on. A new shift replaced the old, but Nebam remained supervising the work, and Retza with him, making sure he took breaks to drink and eat. The air grew thicker with dust. And the work was slow, moving forward bit by bit, removing the rubble, clearing and repairing the tracks, and shoring up the tunnel with new struts at regular intervals.

Gilarth arrived with the third change of shift. He took

Nebam by the arm. 'This could take days, Secondwun, you need to rest.'

Nebam shook off Gilarth's big hand. 'They might be close.'

'Or not. Take a rest. The Lead Hand can direct operations and will send a messenger if anyone is discovered. In the meantime, the Overseer wishes to speak to you.'

The Secondwun rubbed his eyes with grimy hands and allowed Gilarth to lead him to the glimmer trucks. Retza trailed behind Manoah, weariness enfolding him.

The final glance over Retza's shoulder revealed the blue-white beams from the glimmer torch reflecting off the mounds of rubble still blocking the tunnel, almost as though the teams hadn't been digging for sixteen long hours. Whatever happened, this wasn't going to be an easy fix. He hoped Delvina and Zadeki had better success with their mission.

A chill wind buffeted Zadeki, ruffling his feathers and lifting him higher in the sky. Aunt Bikan angled ahead of him, surfing the air currents with a practised ease. Beneath them the great mountain range spread out like a crumpled garment, snowy peaks catching the sunlight in a brilliant white shimmer, in contrast to the grey-blue of the rocky ridges, the yellow-brown plateaus and deep green ravines. A thrill ran through him to the tips of his wings. It was as if he could fly forever, along the mountain ranges to the snow-locked lands in the south.

As the sun moved toward the west, the blue-grey shadows of towering cloud-giants flittered across the land far below. Ahead, the majestic form of Mount Pelee rose up, higher than all the other peaks.

'Almost there,' Aunt Bikan keened.

Zadeki dipped his head in acknowledgement, his sharp eagle-sight catching the green circle, like a hole punched out, further to the south. The Cauldron. As they swooped down into its maw, another eagle rose up towards them.

'Josenif.' Zadeki was overjoyed to see his older brother.

'Well met, da-baba's sister, younger brother. The Kinleader is in the tunnels with the Overseer.'

Aunt Bikan managed to convey a frown on her fierce eagle-face. 'Has not Matu returned to the Great Forest already?'

'Developments have kept her here a little longer. Come, I'll take you to her.'

They landed in the clearing in front of the tunnel entrance. New snow lay in the higher crevices. More trees had been ripped up, more dirt plundered, but no Darane workers were in sight and shovels and lift-bars and pickaxes lay scattered about as though abandoned in the middle of the shift. A few stumps still smouldered, wisps of grey smoke rising in the still air of the Cauldron.

Zadeki changed shape as he landed, his feet hitting the ground in a run. Josenif led them through the tunnels, along a strangely quiet and empty Great Causeway, up the stairs to the Havilah's offices. The watchers flanking the door waved them in.

Gilarth, Da-Matu, old Barekia and Havilah huddled over the copper foil maps and diagrams spread out on the operations table. Nebam sat on a stool to one side, his face grey with fatigue, pale eyes ringed in rock dust and staring at the wall. A runner hovered near the door. There was a taste of desperation in the room though its cause was not obvious.

Da-Matu turned and beckoned. 'Now that was quick, Josenif. Good, we need to speak with you, eldest daughter. How do your negotiations proceed with the children of Tamrak?'

Aunt Bikan pulled her tari tighter around her and inclined her head. 'Good and not so good. The Tamrin have agreed to provide food and send it by yarma train on the King's road, but only once the harvest is in progress.'

Havilah rolled up the map in her hand, the lines etched more deeply in her tired face. 'You can't persuade them to send it sooner?'

'No, they would not shift on that point. It doesn't leave much margin, yet it will still arrive at the Gate before your food runs out.'

Havilah pushed a strand of grey hair from her face. 'Then we have a problem.'

'Just a little.' Nebam's face twisted and he punched his hand. 'The new tunnel collapsed. We've got teams clearing the debris, running shifts back to back.' He swallowed. 'We haven't found any survivors as yet. Either way, it's going to delay completion.'

A grim silence settled in the room, the reason for the pall over the earthbiters now obvious. But surely, it was just a setback. There had to be something they could do.

'Couldn't Baba and the others fly the food up from the Gate to the Cauldron?' Zadeki asked.

Da-Matu gave him a wan smile. 'It's possible, young Zadeki. And we can search for a path suitable for laden yarmas to the Cauldron. Either way, transporting the food the extra distance will add precious time. We should find alternatives.'

Havilah stiffened. 'We can't leave the mountain, if that is what you imply. How many would die in their weakened state. Can't you insist the Tamrin send food now?'

Da-Matu spread out her hands. 'Peace, earth sister. If the yarmas can't make the journey, then it would be foolishness for your people to try. There may be other ways to open the Gate.'

'My toolwuns have already died trying,' Nebam growled, grey eyes flashing. 'There are seven gates, each a lek apart, each massive, each guarded with deadly traps. We haven't even breeched the first gate. My crews will clear the tunnel, we'll get to the outside by the time the food arrives, we will survive. What other option is there?'

'If we had the Overseer's seal, then the gates would swing open to us,' Barekia said in a quiet voice.

'Brilliant, just brilliant. If we had the seal ... but we don't. It was lost with the Old Overseer who his former buddy Gilarth has failed to find.'

Zadeki tensed at the escalating tension in the Secondwun's tone.

Gilarth cleared his throat. 'With respect, Secondwun, there are many, many lek of tunnels for the Old Guard to hide in, nor do I have the watchers to resume searching.'

Nebam swung to face the big watcher. 'Then you can stop sending them to babysit me. Or maybe you can order them to interrogate Uzza's brats. In fact, maybe high and mighty Zara could open the Gate for us.'

'Without that girl, the Crystal Heart would be dead.'

'So you say! You favour her—.'

Gilarth's face mottled. 'Oh, and meanwhile your brother sits consequence-free, unharmed, and well fed after all the carnage he caused.'

'Be quiet!' Havilah thumped the table. 'Be quiet, before I throw you both in the holding cells.'

Both men turned and stared at the Overseer, jaws dropped. Gilarth recovered first, looking shamefaced. 'My apologies, your Honour.'

Nebam folded his arms tight then sighed. 'This is all my fault anyway. If I hadn't pushed to go so fast.'

'We are all under pressure,' Havilah said, touching her throat. 'The stakes are high and our options shrinking.'

Zadeki shivered. It had seemed so easy, to come and help his friends, yet as soon as they solved one problem another appeared, like leaping from one fragile, breaking branch to another.

'Then, can no one else open the gate?' he asked.

All eyes focused on him and he squirmed.

Barekia's bright eyes lit up. 'What about the Sea Dragon King? Surely he could.'

'Yes!' Zadeki pumped a fist. Hadn't Delvina suggested something similar?

'But at what price?' The Kinleader said, echoing Aunt Bikan's words.

'If there is a way to bypass the seal, the Vaane would know it.' Aunt Bikan moved closer to Zadeki. 'Jasalim Pathfinder says the White Ships are still delayed. If he is in need, the Sea Dragon may be open to negotiate.'

'They will want the mines back,' Havilah said.

'Maybe. Or at least access to them. But we were able to negotiate a deal for the Filane and so far the present King has kept it,' Da-Matu said.

'Then perhaps we should find out,' Havilah said. 'Could you help us, Kinleader Telsima, once more?'

Da-Matu's eyes turned inward for a moment, before bowing with hands on chest. 'I fear the road ahead is rocky, but your situation is indeed dire. For your sake, we will take your people as far as Redhaven. But in all your dealings with the Sea Dragon King's followers, be wary.'

Zadeki stilled. Redhaven on the edge of the great ocean and the Sea Dragon's foothold on the wide land. What wonders would await there? What dangers? He only hoped he wouldn't be left behind.

Retza rolled his shoulders to remove the kinks from his neck. He kicked the side of the corridor. Sleep was patchy last shift, full of images of fallen rocks, bodies and strange beasts. There was a sombre mood in the tunnels. Toolwuns walked with eyes to the ground, faces grim. It was everyone's constant nightmare, to be buried in a rockfall. That's how his parents had died, in one of the deepest levels of the realm, when he and Delvina were littlewuns. He could remember his matu's face in dreams and his father's voice, but try as hard as he could, he could never do so awake.

'Retza.' The voice seemed to echo down the tunnel. Retza stopped and scrubbed his face. With Delvina gone, he felt like a hoist without a counterweight. She'd be back soon enough, and then he'd have to decide whether to forgive her for abandoning him. Who was he kidding? He'd be glad to see her.

'Retza, wait up.' The sound of running feet, light steps and a long-legged stride. He turned just as Zadeki loped up and gave him a rib-crushing hug.

'Hey, I was sorry to hear about the cave-in.'

Retza eased himself out and took a step back. What's with all this touchy-feely stuff? A smile tugged at the corner of his lips. He looked past Zadeki down the long corridor. 'So, is Delvina with you?'

'She's back in Tarka with Danel and the others. Just Aunt Bikan and I came. We're going back again at dawn.'

Retza swallowed down the sour taste. 'I best be going then. I'm on duty soon.'

'Wait a bit.' Zadeki offered him a folded piece of paper. 'A message from Delvina.'

Retza glared at it. So, what was she going to say? 'Sorry for leaving. I'm having a great time.'

'She said, tell him I'm sorry for going like that.' Zadeki shrugged. 'I told her not to worry. People go on journeys all the time, right?'

'You people might. Delvina and I stick together. It's what we do, or at least it was.'

'Of course, you're family. You're needed here, and she's needed there. And when the task is over she'll come back here. Not the end of the world.'

If only it was that easy. Maybe it was for the abovegrounders. 'I have to get to my shift.' He mumbled and strode down the corridor.

'I'll walk with you.'

'I guess she'll be home in a few days. Anyhow, it's not that I miss her. She's just my sister.'

'Oh, the trip to Redhaven is likely to take longer, up to two ten-days before the time we get back.'

Redhaven! And a whole roster or more. Not that he cared. 'Where's this Redhaven?'

'On the coast, it's the main harbour for the ships that sail between the Wide Land and the Lonely Isles. What message should I return to Del? Or, if you like, I can swing by your crib and pick it up before I leave in the morning.'

'Tell her ...' He rubbed the wisps of hair on his chin. 'That being a watcher is grand.' He stopped and grabbed

Zadeki's arm. 'You make sure nothing happens to her, alright.'

Zadeki's dark eyebrows shot up. 'Of course, I will. Everything will be fine. You'll see.'

Retza growled under his breath. Easy enough for him to say. Who knew what dangers lurked beneath the terrifying blue abyss. Though he had to admit, staying here wasn't all that safe either with ever-growing threats, rockfalls, tunnel collapses, riots and starvation. But at least he understood those dangers.

Retza held the paper tighter in his hand. 'I'll write a message for her before you go.'

Both their lives were becoming more uncertain by the day and who knew when they would see each other again.

The horizon star hung in the blue haze of mountains in the west, the sky a luminous blue-green edging into purple. Delvina wandered over the paved space, plaza as the Tamrin called it, in front of the Palace. A sharp breeze from the snow-capped peaks blew strands of hair across her face. It carried heady floral scents, the aromas of roasting meats and a chill bite from the snow-capped peaks.

Delvina reached the end of the square where a wide paved road, now wreathed in blue shadows, cut a path toward the strangely shaped temple. She turned and paced back toward the huge Palace crouching against the darkening sky. Stars winked awake across the amethyst expanse.

'You know, you're right, this is the best time to brave the outside,' Danel's voice broke into her thoughts. He pulled the borrowed Tamrin cloak tighter. 'It is getting a bit chilly now though.'

'I guess.' Though she wasn't ready to go inside to the hustle and noise of the palace.

In the east, the dark shape of two eagles hovered high against the residual glow in the sky. They were big enough to be the shapeshifter Folk. One peeled away and veered toward the orange-gold glow of the watch fire on the observation shelter favoured by the Forest Folk. The other continued flying in their direction. Swooping down and landing in front of them, the bird changed into a familiar shape.

'Zadeki!' Delvina grinned, a light feeling bubbling up inside.

Zadeki smiled back, though his dark eyes remained grave. 'Delvina. Come to the lookout. We have messages for you both, and Aunt Bikan needs to speak to you Danel.'

Delvina sobered at the solemn undertone. 'Is something wrong?'

Zadeki handed her a rolled copper foil as they walked toward the hill the Forest Folk favoured. 'Retza says, "Being a Watcher is grand." Though it also seems to make him grouchy.'

Danel gurgled. 'Having Gilarth as your Lead might make anyone grouchy.'

Zadeki grinned back. 'He is a touch intimidating.' He wrapped his sarum tighter around him and strode towards the firelight in the tree-filled darkness. In the distance a strange bird gave a long mournful hoot.

Which was funny, because Zadeki could be downright scary at times. She hastened to catch up to his long stride.

'Did you tell Havilah we made a deal?'

Zadeki smiled back at her, though it seemed tentative

and uncertain. 'Yes though our news in return is not as good.'

'Is Retza alright?' Visions of the riot they'd been caught up in flooded her mind. But Javot and Putarn were in the holding cells. Though others could still stir up trouble.

'No, nothing like that. He's fine. Says he misses you.'

She snorted. 'Reckon he didn't.'

'Well, not in so many words, but that's what he meant.'

And maybe he did. Delvina sighed. It would be good to get home to the tunnels, even if it required joining the watchers. It felt strange not to have Retza at her side, restraining her wilder impulses and ready to defend her against any comer. She jumped as the bush beside her rustled with some small night creature.

They arrived at the top of the hill. Highwun Bikan stopped speaking to Jasalim and a couple of Forest Folk Delvina didn't recognise. She pulled a small copper foil out of her tari and passed it to Danel. 'From Overseer Havilah, Speaker Danel.'

Danel moved closer to the fire, unrolled and scanned the inscribed message, his face stiffening.

'So, what's happened?' Delvina whispered to Zadeki.

Zadeki took a deep breath. 'The tunnel collapsed. Half the Greenstone South are trapped beneath the rubble. It could take days to clear it.'

It felt as though she was breathing underwater. Greenstone South. Her old crew, her parents' crew. Another thought surfaced. Days! Maybe longer. 'And it still mightn't be safe. Without the tunnel we won't be able to get the food to the people in time.'

'Nebam thinks it salvageable.'

Danel looked up, his face a mask, and passed the message to Delvina. 'Narval will stay here to help organise the delivery of the food. You are to come with me to Redhaven, to find answers about the Gate from the Vaane.'

Delvina swallowed hard. More wonders to explore, yet she was eager to return home and see Retza again. She forced back the tears. This journey wasn't about her curiosity or desire to see beyond the caverns. The Overseer trusted her and Danel to find answers that might make the difference between life and death for her people. She'd travel twice as far if that's what it took. Though she had no idea how they were to get there.

Zadeki hooked his arm around the prow of the boat made of bundled reeds, legs dangling against the side. Mist rose off the grey water like smoke and rolled out over the high banks of the river. He wrinkled his nose at the rank river smells of waterweed and the acrid bite of smoke from the village cooking fires. Argenti's silver half circle smiled serenely at the pinnacle of the sky, with Alumi's golden crescent not far behind. Like a reflection, a faint promise of light bordered on the horizon.

The Tamrin's reed boats were bigger than the canoes his Kin fashioned in the Great Forest, though Da-Baba said the White Ships were larger again.

'Aren't you afraid of falling, youngwun?' a deep voice came from behind him.

Zadeki twisted around and grinned up at Danel. The Thirdwun stood with strong legs planted on the reed deck, his thick fingers wrapped around a steaming mug. The rich velvet aroma of hot koka drifted toward him.

'I suppose you can turn into a fish.' Danel grumped, as he settled down on a pile of coiled rope.

'No, but I can swim like one.' Zadeki looked down at the grey water bubbling beside the curved prow and shrugged. The current was strong here, a relentless pull to the ocean, yet he'd grown up swimming in the rivers of the Forest. 'This is better than being trapped inside stone buildings or pinned down under the bulk of the mountain. Would you have preferred to fly the whole way to Redhaven?'

'No!' Danel looked pained. 'I'd probably sink like a counterweight here as much as in the air, but at least I'm not clinging on in fear of my life.'

Zadeki yawned and stretched, keeping his balance on the gunnels. He'd enjoyed the flights from Tarka, across the high mountains to the lowlands in the west. But this was exhilarating too. Baba had stretched out the distance he could carry the Darane, using the terrain, maximising use of the thermals and the koraktil's ability to glide long distances, so it had been a short walk to the Tamrin settlement in the river valley where the rivers met. Once shown Supak Kapok's ring and message, the watermen readily agreed to take them to Redhaven.

'So why can't you turn into a fish?'

Zadeki laughed. The peals echoed over the still water and bounced off the steep valley slopes. He slapped his hand over his mouth and glanced at the sleepers under the shelter mid-deck.

Delvina stirred, tossing her head from side to side. Baba lay in a deep sleep unmoving, still recuperating from his last flight. Aunt Bikan stood at the stern in low conversation with the head waterman.

Zadeki lowered his voice. 'Most fish are too small and tiny-brained a form to risk.'

Danel grunted 'Well, I don't understand any of it.' He

took another cautious sip of his thick drink. 'Though this brown stuff is liquid gold.'

The sky lightened to a pearlescent grey, soft light glimmering on the patchwork of fields on the flats and climbing up the slopes of the shallow river-valley. The water sprung alight with silver-fire as the sun peeped over the distant mountain ranges behind them. It would be another warm day, unlike the chilly snow-edged days in the mountains.

'No,' Delvina muttered. She rolled over. 'No! Don't!'

Danel frowned. 'She's not sleeping well.'

Zadeki swung his legs into the boat, dropped onto the deck and ran lightly to the shelter. He knelt beside her and shook her shoulder. With the touch of her skin, an intense feeling of darkness and sorrow hit him like a slap. It was no wonder given all that had happened that she carried such heavy burdens.

Delvina stirred and sat up. She looked straight at him and recognition seeped into her clear grey eyes. A soft smile tugged at her lips. 'Zadeki.'

She rubbed a pale hand over her white-gold hair. The soft light picked out the scattering of freckles across her snub nose and glinted off her light eyelashes. Zadeki let his hand drop to his side. He'd promised Retza he'd protect her. And he would as his own sister.

'Here, some of this koka stuff will help.' Danel thrust a mug at her.

'Thanks.' Delvina dipped her head and took the drink. 'Just a stupid dream.'

'Sometimes the Maker speaks to us in dreams. Can you remember what they were?'

Delvina took a sip, her cheeks pinking. 'Lots of stuff.' She swirled the koka, eyes large. 'Hunger. Pain. Water in waves and ... and you ...' Her voice dwindled away. She shook her heard. 'Like I said silly things.'

'I was in your dream?'

Pink flared to red. 'Yes, no, I'm not sure. A strange white bird with narrow wings far too long, trapped in a dark pit with a broken wing and ...' She shook her head as if freeing herself from spider silk. 'It's fading and anyhow, it doesn't make any sense.'

Zadeki rubbed his nose. His arm hairs rose and a feeling of unease shivered through him, like a river breeze ruffling the calm surface of the water. Was it memory or premonition or warning or none of those things? 'Dreams can be important. You should tell Aunt Bikan or Baba. She may know what it means.'

Delvina shook her head, lips tight. 'No, please don't. It doesn't mean anything. It was just a dream. Just the day we met, when you broke your wing.'

Perhaps. He wasn't sure.

Sweat beaded Delvina's face and she was thankful for the cloth shelter in the middle of this strange boat made of reeds. The sun had burned off the mist, leaving a day of breathless heat. The valley sides slid beside them at times dipping down to reveal rolling plains of dry brush and grass. In the sky, birds, smaller versions of the bird-shape Zadeki's Kin preferred, floated above the Tamrin settlements. Zadeki said they were kites.

After a couple of days, a few more tributaries, the river widened out into a broad brown flood. The taciturn watermen who spoke a few words of Eldar said the river would swell to twice this size once the snows melted and the rains swept into the mountains from the east.

Dreams continued to trouble her. Dreams of Zadeki and flying, dreams that always started pleasant but soon twisted into a sense of danger and disaster, though on waking the details had slipped back into the mists of her mind. So much had happened, so many had died or been injured, one at least by her own hands, and the threat of starvation and disaster for her people was still real. Once all her people wanted to do was shut the doors to the outside world, to depend on no one else but themselves. Now, if they didn't work out how to open the gate, they could all die. And maybe that was a good thing—the opening of the gate, not the dying. The sooner they got to Redhaven the better.

'A feather for your thoughts,' Zadeki grinned at her, twirling a brilliant red and green feather between his supple fingers. He offered it to her and sat beside her.

'Wondering how Retza and the others are doing.'

She moved a little closer to him, his presence easing the tightness in her muscles, if not the tempo of her heartbeat.

Zadeki wasn't looking at her, leaning forward, gaze fixed ahead. Something had caught his attention on the distant horizon, though all she could see was the brown, water rushing and rippling under the flat expanse of the sky.

He jumped up in a sudden lithe movement and punched both fists into the air. 'Woohoo! White buildings. I see white building. I think we've arrived.'

He stretched out a long arm to Delvina. She took it and he pulled her to her feet. She stared at the horizon, her eyes watering at the glare of sunlight bouncing off the river.

Highwun Bikan turned from her conversation with Korak and shielded her eyes. 'The youngling might be right.'

Zadeki gave a lopsided grin. 'Let's hope the Vaane can help you with your dilemma.'

Danel sat up from a doze, his brown hair sticking out at different angles. 'Will one of you fly ahead? To let them know we're coming?'

'Better we stay together. And an element of surprise may work in our favour.' Bikan turned to Zadeki. 'You know how the Sea Dragon King feels about shape-shifting.'

Zadeki brow's crinkled. 'Yes. I won't forget, Da-Ba-sestru.'

Korak clapped him on the shoulder. 'Good. Though father's sister, I'm sure the Vaane already know we're coming.'

'I think being able to change shape is a wonderful gift. I wish I could do it.' Delvina felt her face burn. Why had she said that? She had never imagined the world was so big, so full of colour and life. It made her feel so small and insignificant. But it was true. To be able to fly like Zadeki or Korak, to see the world through different eyes …

Highwun Bikan gave her a warm smile. 'Not many think like you.' She opened her mouth as if to say more, then closed it.

A gust of wind brought a strange smell on the wind, salty and a little rank, and thunder boomed in a low rumble though the bronzed blue sky remained empty of all but the wispiest of clouds.

The river widened out into what looked like a huge lake, though the water broke up in foam-tipped triangular peaks. A strong wind blew in from the west. Overhead silver-grey birds cawed in a rowdy commotion. They wheeled and swooped, dipping yellow beaks in the

water and bringing up flapping silver fish. Adobe huts
clustered on the cliffs on the north side of this strange
lake, while buildings of white marble adorned the gentler
slope to the south.

'The village of Akra to the north,' Highwun Bikan
pointed. 'The Sea Dragon King's Redhaven to the south.'

The briny wind stung Delvina's eyes. The strange
thunder grew louder, swelling and receding, capturing
the rhythm of her heartbeat. Boom, boom. Boom, boom.
Boom, boom, boom.

Beyond two arms of land, the water stretched out to
the horizon, with no visible land to hem it in.

'The ocean.' Zadeki breathed. He leaned over the side
of the boat, his midnight eyes sparkling like a star-
studded sky. 'It's as big as the Great Forest.'

'Bigger,' Highwun Bikan said, an indulgent smile on
her pale lips.

Danel closed his mouth then shook his head. 'The
world is wonderous huge.'

Delvina could only agree and ponder at how much
greater the Maker of all this would be.

The watermen adjusted the steering paddle and the
wind caught the square sail at the stern. The boat
skipped through rough water, tipping from side to side
and up and down in a most unnerving way.

Up ahead, a white stone wall rushed toward them. A
huge boat with a steep-sided white hull bobbed against
the wall to one side. Strung up on poles on its decking,
wings of cloth rippled in the stiff breeze. Further back,
white buildings towered above them like jagged cliffs or
teeth in an oldwun's mouth. Delvina's stomach muscles
tensed and she gripped the gunnels, waiting for the
wooden boat to crash into the wall.

Instead, the watermen adjusted the sail and tilted the steering oar. The boat slowed and turned in a graceful circle. The Tamrin watermen rushed to the left side, throwing thick ropes at the people standing ready on the wall.

Only once the boat was secured, did Delvina look up the hill. She sucked in her breath. The buildings made of creamy marble, sculpted and shaped into ethereal shapes and with blue-tiled roofs, clustered on the slopes of the cliff. Gardens with shrubs, trees and flowers were arranged—not with the geometrical balance of the Palace gardens, but in an artful and surprising ways. Statues and windchimes, water fountains and murals were scattered about. If Tarka had been solid and monumental, reminding Delvina of the bulky mountains, these buildings recalled the sky, wind and forest in their shapes. Built of stone and clay tiles, the structures displayed a natural grace that followed the lines of the valley. The settlement could have grown into the side of the valley.

A round tower, like the trunk of one of the giant trees she'd seen on her visit to the forest, reared up closer to the sound of the ... ocean, she guessed it was. And beside it was a bigger building about half the size of the Tamrin Palace but adorned with a domed roof and smaller towers and arches. Flags fluttered in the wind. Yet the paved streets and vibrant gardens seemed empty.

'So, is that a White Ship?' Danel asked, pointing to the other boat secured to the wall.

Highwun Bikan touched her chin. 'Yes, though it looks old, and there is only one.'

'What do we do now?" Danel asked.

'We wait.'

Delvina heaved a sigh. Again. More waiting. More talking. Hopefully the Vaane would heed their pleas and be willing to help them.

Retza trudged back to the watchers' ward room, glad that another long shift helping the crews assigned to clear the cave-in was over. His feet and back ached and his hair and eyes were clogged with rock dust. He felt too tired to eat, but hopefully the washrooms would be free and he could sink into a steaming bath.

As he hooked his token on the duty board, Gilarth stepped out of the inner office.

'Watcher Retza, just about to send for you. Come in, talk with me.'

Retza's stomach clenched. Was he in trouble? He ignored the smirks and curious looks from his fellow watchers and followed Gilarth into the room.

Gilarth sank into his chair behind a broad desk and waved Retza to sit on one of the stools. 'How are the rescue operations going?'

Retza made a sour face then he remembered who he was talking to. Straightening his jerkin, he said 'No change, sir. Maybe another half lek cleared. It's slow progress.'

'Yeah,' Gilarth glowered. 'Taking up a lot of work shifts.'

'It's still possible the toolwuns are alive.' Retza could hear the lack of conviction in his own voice.

Searching for survivors, meant going slow and careful. Only this morning, he'd heard Gregan was demanding more crews for the farms. But he understood why Nebam wasn't ready to give up on their former crib mates.

Gilarth ran a large hand over his craggy face. 'Aye. Never mind. It's not as if there's time to start a new tunnel. That's Nebam and Havilah's business. I'm shifting you back to guarding Lady Zara.'

Retza suppressed a groan. 'Sir, why me? She said barely a word. Mostly I saw her back.'

Gilarth grunted. 'She's stubborn. Reminds me of another young female, I once knew well.'

'Sir?'

'Never mind. We're running out of time, Watcher. If Nebam's tunnel doesn't work or Thirdwun Danel doesn't get information from these Vaane, the Tamrin's food shipment might as well be back at Tarka for all the good it will do.'

'If I know Delvina, she won't leave till she has what we need.'

A surprised chuckle escaped Gilarth. He shook his head. 'Maybe. But I'll be more comfortable with more than one option. If Zara knows anything about the gate or even where her baba would have gone to ground, we need to know. And if she doesn't cooperate, Nebam will soon be pressing me to persuade her with sterner methods.'

'But, she is bounded to the Crystal Heart.' And without the Heart, none of it mattered.

'True ... and I don't intend to let her be harmed on my watch.' Gilarth drummed his fingers on the desk. 'I've known her since she took her first steps. Maybe it doesn't look that way, but she has a soft spot for you.'

Retza studied his hands, nicked and grimy from the rescue efforts. Gilarth must be half-crazed with lack of sleep. 'If you say so.' He caught a glimpse of Gilarth's knowing gaze. Orders were orders but pandering to Uzza's daughter while there was still an outside chance for his former crib mates stuck in his gullet. 'They could still be alive,' he blurted.

'After ten-day and how could they be under so much rock? Only Nebam thinks so.'

'But if they are?' Had his parents been abandoned to their fate too? Da-Baba had always been cagey on the details. No, that was silly. They weren't under the same pressures then. 'You are so quick to defend Zara. Is it because Greenstone South are toolwuns, you are so ready to abandon them to die?'

Gilarth shifted in his chair and looked away. The stylus snapped in his hand. The dik dak dik dak of the timepiece on the wall counted the moments. Gilarth placed the two broken pieces of the stylus on the desk, his face a mask.

Retza's pulse ratchetted upwards. What was he thinking, blabbing off like that?

'Sorry, sir,' Retza mumbled. 'That was out of line.'

'Yes, it was.' Gilarth glared at him. 'You belonged to Greenstone South, didn't you?'

'At least four or more generations, sir.'

Gilarth stood, placed his hands on the table, and leaned forward. 'Right, Watcher Retza. You get to stay with the rescue crews five more days. Then I'm transferring you to guard Zara. You got any objections to that?'

'No, sir.'

'Good, then dismissed.'

Retza bolted out of the room before the big Watcher changed his mind.

Zadeki stood entranced as the reed boat rocked beneath his feet. He often heard Da-Matu and others' tales of the Lonely Isles, now he was tasting something of their wonders with his own eyes.

Baba draped his arm around Zadeki's back. 'Don't be beguiled by outward beauty, son of my heart.'

In other words, be on guard. The Vaane were not their friends. Zadeki took a deep breath and jumped over the side of the reed boat. He circled around the Tamrin watermen, unloading the boat of barrels and boxes of produce, and joined the rest of his group standing on the far edge of the wharf.

'This is magnificent.' Danel rubbed his nose, red and flaking a little from excess sunburn despite coatings of Aunt Bikan's plant juice. He swivelled in a slow circle, grey eyes staring.

'But where is everyone?' Delvina hoisted the small pack she acquired in Tarka over her shoulder. 'Shouldn't we let the Vaane know we've arrived, Highwun Bikan?'

'They know already, daughter of the mountain,' Aunt Bikan said, an intense watchfulness underlying her calm demeanour.

Zadeki's muscles coiled. He could feel hostile eyes watching and evaluating them. The Vaane were not their friends, reverberated in his head.

The leader of the watermen approached Aunt Bikan. 'Wise one, we'll unload the boat and sign off with the Harbour Master.'

'When do you head back?'

'Tomorrow morning, with the advantage of the two-new-moon tide and morning sea breeze. Will you require a berth?'

'Our business may take longer. I'll send a message if we need to return with you.'

'As you wish.' The Tamrin bowed and joined his companions.

'Someone is coming,' Baba said.

Zadeki could hear pounding of many feet on stone approaching. Moments later, a squad of lithe warriors in black leather and silver helms appeared from behind one of the bigger buildings and quickly surrounded them. A stately woman in a flowing robe adorned with gold thread stepped out from between them. Rich-brown eyes bristling with suspicion swept over them.

'What is your business at Redhaven, Flame-get? And be warned, our archers have bows notched and aimed should you attempt any treachery.'

A sudden salt-laden wind buffeted them. Aunt Bikan smoothed down a fold in her tari and tented her hands on her breast.

'Greetings, Harbour Master Rebekka. We seek an audience with the Warden of Redhaven on behalf of Darian's children.'

The willowy woman's koka-brown hair lifted in the salt-laden wind and her red-brown eyes bored into Aunt Bikan. 'The treaty forbids your presence in our cities, daughter of Telsima.'

'It grants us right of audience. The Sea Dragon King would be interested in what the mountain dwellers have to offer.'

Rebekka scrutinised each of them with a piercing stare. Zadeki's neck crawled and his mind resisted when he felt the gentle probe of her thoughts. Her gaze shifted to the Darane and her fine lips curled. 'Why would rebel ebed, mere servants, be of any interest to us?'

'This is what we would discuss with the Warden.'

'We shall see.' The Harbour Master touched the

flower-shaped crystal at her neck, her eyes focusing on a distant point.

Zadeki stifled his breathing. Would the Vaane help his friends?

Rebekka's fingers dropped from the crystal pendant. 'The Warden will speak with the ebed. You may leave them with me.' She beckoned to Danel and Delvina.

Zadeki bristled. 'We're not leaving our friends undefended.'

The wind dropped. The watchers lowered their spears. On balconies and rooftops, archers moved into sight, bows drawn. Zadeki, Aunt Bikan and Baba moved closer around Danel and Delvina, facing outward. Every sense intensified; the sound of lapping water against the dock, the raucous cries of the seagulls and the shouts of the waterman, the thump of stores hitting the wharf, the sting of salt, the stench of seaweed and rotting fish, the ominous creak of bowstrings.

Rebekka held up a hand. 'If you want to speak to the Warden, you need to come with me.'

'Not without our friends.' Delvina clenched her fists, a short bundle of defiance.

'Your 'friends' are not welcome here.'

Danel wavered, then swallowed, squared his shoulders, stood straighter. 'Then perhaps the Warden could speak to us on the Tamrin boat.'

Harbourmaster Rebekka pressed her lips together. 'I doubt it.' She touched the crystal. A moment later she spoke. 'The Warden will allow the Flame-get to come with you, though we recommend you reconsider your guides in the future. Now don't try our patience any further. Come.'

She spun around, and the watchers parted to allow

her to walk along the paved road leading up the slope to the domed building on top of the hill. Danel and Delvina, with a nervous glance at Bikan, followed. Zadeki fell in behind them. And the watchers closed in behind them. Zadeki could imagine their hot breath and the sharp point of their spears hurrying them along.

Sunlight fell in golden showers around him, reflecting off the polished stone buildings and fountains and statues. They passed a lithe woman with red-brown skin and silver hair, clipping away at a bush. Her eyes widened, and she ducked behind a stone column. Other watchful eyes followed them.

Zadeki's muscles tingled with the urge to change into the jaguar or eagle form. He'd thought Aunt Bikan exaggerated the prejudice of the Vaane towards his Kin, the hate and danger. Surely after all these ten-years of uneasy peace, an understanding had been built. But this felt like walking into a lightly sprung trap with any hope of escape barred against them.

Danel cast his eyes around, taking in the delicate stone work of the airy room with rows of slender columns and arched windows along both sides. Plants and even small trees seemed to grow out of the stone floor and long trails of leaves and flowers hung from balconies above them. Nothing had prepared him for buildings that mimicked gardens. Just when he thought he could not be awed again, another wonder left him struggling to speak. Like a jaguar, here beauty and gracefulness of form also hid danger. Was there any reason these people would help them? He only hoped that he wouldn't let Havilah and the Glittering Realm down.

The silvery sound of a bell sounded and the bifold doors at the other end of the hall swung open. Harbour Master Rebekka ushered them into a circular room where a large stone-carved lizard with wide crest and webbed feet spouted a stream of water at its centre. Fish and birds cavorted around it. While similar to the Tamrin fountains, the detail here was exquisite.

Two tall silver-skinned beardless men stood talking together in serious tones. The taller one in long sapphire blue robes. His thin austere face was turned toward them, framed by long black hair threaded with silver grey. The other not quite as tall and stockier in long tunic, breeches and high boots stepped back into an alcove.

Rebekka placed her palms together and bowed. 'Here are the intruders, I mentioned, Warden Ealam.'

'Thank you, Harbour Master Rebekka.' His eyes lingered over Danel, seeming to peel away the layers of his soul with a pickaxe, then shifted to Delvina, his long nose wrinkling. The Warden spread his long fingers in a fan, pressing them together. 'I have never seen ebed so pale. Are you sure they are Darian's people, Shapeshifter? I thought those renegades well and truly dead and buried deep in the mines by now.'

Danel's hands clenched at the dismissive tone. 'We are very much alive and live as a free people.'

'Then why are you here wasting my time? I have more important things to concern myself with. Harbour Master, escort these rebels out of Redhaven.' Ealam turned back to the other man waiting to one side. 'Go on Mariner. How soon can you leave?'

The Mariner stroked his cleft chin. 'We can cast off on this afternoon's double-moon tide, your Honour.'

Danel blinked, his feet seemingly taken root to the floor. Dismissed out of hand. Not even heard. It wasn't possible!

Rebekka sniffed. 'Shall we remove the riff-raff, sir?'

'You will need to remove us first,' Korak's voice deepening into a jaguar-like growl.

The Forest Folk, bristling with unleashed power, closed in a semi-circle around Danel and Delvina. The Watchers edged closer, hands on batons and metal weapons.

Ealam swung back to face them, his nostrils flared. 'Traitors helping traitors, why am I not surprised.'

'That, son of Lotah, depends on how you look at it.' Highwun Bikan held up a hand. She gave a sour smile. 'So, the reports are true. The white ships haven't come? Besides, how is the supply of the earth's riches in the Lonely Isles these days?'

'What do you know of that?'

'As much as you, it would seem. You would do well to listen to Darian's folk, they have come a long way to speak to you.'

'Tell them we're not going until we have been heard.' Delvina hissed in Danel's ear.

Runner Delvina and Highwun Bikan were right. They hadn't come all this way to be ignored. He took a deep breath and tugged his jerkin. Ignoring his treacherous knees, he stepped forward, trusting the Forest Folk to keep the watchers off his back.

'Sir, Your Honour, I am Speaker Danel, sister's son to Overseer Havilah. It is vital we speak to you. The least you could do is have the courtesy to hear us.'

Ealam's jet-black eyes fixed on Danel. His eyes were as dark as Zadeki's, but instead of reflecting light, they seemed to swallow it. 'This Overseer Havilah is the traitor Hezikah's daughter?'

Danel swallowed hard. Focus on the facts. 'No, your Honour. We deposed Hezikah's son, Uzza six rosters ago. The new Overseer, Havilah, sent us with an offer. She wishes to reopen the Gate and the Glittering Realms.'

'I thought the mines were played out.'

'Not at all, your Honour. We are willing to exchange valuables for your help.' Danel dug a hand into his pouch and opened his fingers. Sunlight faceted off the gems on his calloused palm.

'Pretty baubles.' Warden Ealam tucked his hands behind him, but his eyes gleamed. 'Show me.'

Danel passed the pouch's mixture of precious stones and crystals into Ealam's hands. 'This is just a sample, Highwun.'

'You can get more of these?' The Warden held up the one uncut glimmer crystal to the light. 'Bigger perhaps?'

Danel took the glittering gem and held it. 'The lode veins are at the deepest levels and dangerous. But it can be done.' Or at least he hoped so after all these years.

The Warden paused, then beckoned. 'Very well, explain what it is you want.'

Danel motioned for Delvina to take the cylinder to Warden Ealam. The tall man pulled out the message and unrolled it. 'Do you know the contents? Explain it to me.'

Perhaps this wasn't going to be so hard after all. 'We require knowledge of the Overseer's seal of authority. How it might be transferred or overcome, or perhaps a new seal made so we can open the Gate.'

Ealam allowed the message foil to flutter to the ground. 'Very touching, and I see here your situation is dire indeed, but I can't help you. We are just a forgotten outpost here.' Bitterness tinged his voice.

'Nonsense.' Highwun Bikan crossed her arms, her dark eyes flashing. 'Warden of the White Ships, you can request information from the Lonely Isles. Perhaps, the Custodian of the King's library in Silantis could help.'

Danel shifted uneasily. How long would that take? Already thirteen days had passed since they'd left home.

Warden Ealam's mouth twisted, as though tasting something sour. 'Yes, there would be answers there, but I'm not a farspeaker any more than I am a crystal singer or technician.'

Highwun Bikan seemed to swell in size. 'You equivocate. One gifted in farspeaking, such as Harbour Master Rebekka, can use the Towers of Speaking.' She pointed to the spire visible through a line of arched windows.

'No doubt, but we have not heard from Silantis by Speaking Stone or White Ships for three cycles of the Golden moon. We can't help you. Came back another time.'

Delvina took a step forward, fists clenched. 'Another time will be too late!'

Danel gritted his teeth against the bitter taste of disappointment and a rising anger. Did no one but the Forest Folk care that thousands would die if they didn't get help? There had to be a way.

'What about the ship in the harbour?' Zadeki asked. 'Could that take the Overseer's message.'

Warden Ealam cast him a grim glance. He fingered the glimmer crystal in his hand. 'That old thing ...'

The other man in tunic and breeches cleared his throat. 'The White Rose may be old and designed more for coastal travel, but we've patched her up. More to the point, she's all we've got. I could take these ebed with me on the voyage, Warden.'

Danel quailed. Another journey across the vast ocean and for what purpose, another refusal? Would they be able to return in time? Or return at all? At least he could walk home from here, however long it took. But he could not walk across the oceans or fly like the Forest Folk.

'We have to do whatever it takes,' Delvina whispered, her face grey. She stepped forward and picked up the message foil, rolling it and placing it into the cylinder.

Danel hitched a breath. 'Yes, we will go to Silantis to deliver Overseer Havilah's request.'

The Warden pressed long fingers to his beardless chin. 'That could work. I'll give you the needed clearances and a letter to the Grand Technician and entrust you into Mariner Habbiah's care.'

'Our thanks, your Honour.' He turned to the Forest Folk. 'You have done so much already, I cannot ask you—'

'Nonsense,' Bikan snapped. 'One of us at least must go with you, so the answer can be taken as fast as possible to Havilah. We will come with you.'

'What? You cannot allow that. The Island is forbidden to all Flame-get.' Harbour Master Rebekka said.

Danel's heart crashed to his boots. But if they had to do it without the help of the Forest Folk, they would.

Highwun Bikan folded her arms and glared at the Harbour Master. 'By right of treaty we can address the Sea Dragon King or his representative and successors.'

Mariner Habbiah cleared his throat. 'Your honour, if I might speak. The shapeshifters would solve the problem I mentioned to you. With the Speaking Towers no longer guiding us, we could sail right past the Lonely Isles and into trackless wastes of the ocean. Without the Towers, it will be like searching for a pebble in the sea.'

'How would the Flame-get help?'

'The shifters can fly many lek in either direction, far beyond what our lookouts can see. If they see any sign of land—we will know to head toward it.'

'This requires thought.' The Warden paced about the room, circling the fountain.

'Surely you are not considering this atrocity?' Harbour Master Rebekka demanded.

'It is an extreme measure, but these are extreme times. We can only assume some foul tragedy has befallen our home and it is imperative Mariner Habbiah reaches the island.'

'But Warden!'

'Harbour Master, you forget yourself.' The Warden stopped in front of Danel. 'Very well, take the shapeshifters with you, but do not be surprised if your companions get a cool reception. Now, if you excuse me, I have important matters to attend to. Rebekka will show you a place to wait until it is time to board the ship.'

With a sharp nod, he tucked the pouch of jewels under his robe and walked with the Mariner to the other end of the room, leaving the Harbourmaster fuming beside them.

Delvina moved closer and touched Danel's elbow. 'You did well, Thirdwun.'

Danel smiled at the praise. 'With the help of my friends,' he said. 'Though we still have a long journey ahead of us.' Surely this was the last.

Harbour Master Rebekka glared at them, her beautiful face twisted. 'You got what you wanted, now come with me and I'll find somewhere to stow you until you leave.'

Zara sat huddled on the sleeping mat, hugging her knees. The glimmer lights were dimmed for the third shift and the dregs of a dream sat like curdled milk in her stomach. The dark images full of inky shadows and dead bodies shredded and frayed into the dark corners of the room, their new prison. Her hand brushed her brother's head, his warmth and the soft sigh of his breathing giving her comfort. Jesson was curled up in a tight ball, his face squished up against her.

'Zara.' He mumbled, his eyelids fluttering. 'No, don't hurt her.' His hands clenched into fists and he thrashed against her.

'Hush, Jesson, you're dreaming.' She put her arms around him, stroking his pale sweat drenched hair. 'No need to worry.'

His arm was healing, and he seemed readier to accept their situation, readier to make friends with these rebels, than she was. She shivered and pulled the cover tighter around her shoulders. Something was happening, something bad, but no one seemed keen to tell her. Perhaps their father was regaining the realm and this nightmare would soon be over.

This room was more cramped than the huge Heart Room, though she could still feel the soft hum of the giant crystals vibrate through her, in time with her heartbeat. The tendrils of power reached through the different levels of her father's realm, though she had no idea how to control them or if in fact she could. It was unsettling. Had Baba lived with this night and day for so many solars since Da-Baba's death?

She stiffened at the sound of boots tramping along the corridor outside, the clang of the metal gate, then voices.

The door slipped open and her heart hammered faster. In a flash of memory, she felt Javot's sweaty hands groping her, his hot breath on her face. She pulled Jesson against her, her breath catching.

A dark figure stood in the doorway, eyes gleaming in the faint light. After a moment, her muscles relaxed as she recognised the familiar shape.

'What do you want, traitor?' she spat. He'd promised to protect them, then sided with Havilah. He'd regret his treachery when father returned.

'Checking that you've been provided for, my Lady. Which I see you have.' He took a step back and began to pull the door closed.

'Wait! You could at least tell me what's happening. Why you've imprisoned us here.'

Gilarth hesitated then shrugged. 'For your own protection.'

'There's fighting, then.' Her breath quickened.

'No.' He ran his hand along the door. 'No, the … a tunnel collapsed. And we need as many able-bodied people to clear the rubble while there is a chance of survivors.'

Jesson yawned and sat up. 'They're alive. In the western tunnel.' He blinked his eyes as Gilarth directed a glimmer torch into the boy's face.

'Well, I hope you're right, lad. There have been too many deaths lately.' He stepped back into the room. 'Lady Zara, do you remember your father ever speaking about the seal or … or where he might go if the realm was endangered?'

Fire flashed through Zara. 'You have the gall to ask me? Do you think I would betray him like you have?' Just because she'd helped with the Crystal Heart didn't mean she would help them anymore.

'My lady, you have to accept—'

'No! Don't you dare tell me he is dead. He's alive. I know he is.'

'Even if you are right, the life of everyone in this realm might depend on opening the Gate, including yours and Jesson's.'

She was on her feet before she knew it. 'No one should go through the Gate. My father forbids it, my Da-Baba forbade it. He would have had a good reason to do so. To protect us from danger.'

'That danger was two hundred years ago. It has passed. Now we face new dangers.'

'Because you defied the Dark Ones, refused the sacrifice they demanded.'

'Which ones, my Lady, which youngwuns should we have given up? Delvina or Jesson?'

A shudder ran through her like a ground quake. That wasn't fair.

Gilarth continued, hard and relentless. 'As much as you honour and respect your father, perhaps you should consider he might be wrong. That it is reverence of the Dark Ones that has reduced us to this plight. And that any deliverance that requires the killing of youngwuns is abominable.'

'Get out, get out.' Zara ran at Gilarth, her hands tight balls. He caught her wrists. 'As you wish, my Lady. But if you do think of something ...' With a sharp nod, he let her go and walked out.

She grabbed her shoe and threw it. It bounded off the edge of the closing door.

'Maybe Baba was wrong about the sacrifices, Zara.'

She threw her hands into the air. 'Argh, Jesson. You're too young to understand.'

'But Delvina is our friend.'

'None of these people are our friends.'

'Delvina and Retza and Zadeki all stood up for us against Javot and Putarn.'

There was something in what Jesson said. But, no, if she admitted that one thing, where would it lead?

'Go back to sleep, Jesson.'

'But Zara!'

'Sleep.'

He gave an exaggerated sigh and lay down on his side of the mat. Zara settled down beside him and closed her eyes, but her mind wouldn't turn off as it worried and fretted and turned over and over Gilarth's words and why he was suddenly interested in the seal.

Delvina groaned and clutched her stomach. The constant movement of the ship up and down, up and down, up and down, side to side – tipping and rolling, rolling and tipping—had not stopped since they'd left Redhaven two days ago. The sky was scudded with clouds and the inky blue waves stretched to horizon in every direction. She was glad the Forest Folk had resisted the Mariner's suggestion of accommodation in the hold, for at least on the deck the wind cooled her face and she could contain the nausea. A wayward gust caught the striped shawl the Tamrin had given Delvina to protect her pale skin from the sun, one end pulling free.

Above her the white sails shuddered and filled with wind, pushing the ship through the waves. The workers with skin of various shades from ivory to red-brown, raced across the deck in performance of their tasks. Silver-grey birds of different shapes and sizes swooped and swirled around them like ... snowflakes in the Cauldron. With a groan, she clutched her stomach.

Fingers brushed her arm and she twisted around. Highwun Bikan stood beside her, her eyes concerned, her touch soothing.

'I wish we'd brought some chica root. It would have calmed your stomach, youngling. But this should help.' She held out a beaker of a steaming tisane with a sharp earthy aroma.

Delvina took it and sipped, one hand clutching the rail and both feet planted to ride the unpredictable rolling of the ship.

'Is it always this bad?'

Bikan smiled with compassion. 'A bit blustery, perhaps, but calm enough. Either way, I would prefer to fly.'

Delvina shot the older woman an envious look. None of the Forest Folk seemed affected by the sea malady. Even Danel more or less adjusted after the first couple of days. She just hoped it didn't get any rougher than this.

She glanced toward Zadeki balanced on the prow, eyes fixed on the dolphins surfing in the ship's bow wave. A sleek nose and curved body crested and with a flick of a tail disappeared. Zadeki's dark curls fanned out in the wind and his lean strong body looked as relaxed as if he were in one of the hammocks the Captain had strung up on the deck for them to sleep in. She hoped that she could continue to spend time with him after this adventure. Though she doubted she could persuade Retza that visiting the Forest again would be a good idea.

The ship gave a violent heave. Delvina's feet slid sideways. Highwun Bikan steadied her and took the empty cup. 'Perhaps you should sit down, child.'

Delvina sighed. 'What of Zadeki, won't he fall in?'

Highwun Bikan's angular face quirked into a half-frown, half-smile. 'And if he does ...? He will shapeshift and fly off before he hits the waves. The Maker's gift is strong in Korak's son. It comes easily to him, though that can sometimes be a drawback as much as it's a blessing.'

Delvina frowned. 'We must seem so ordinary and ... well drab to you.' It was no wonder Zadeki didn't really see her.

Bikan touched her arm. 'Forgive me, friend Delvina, if I've given you that impression. The Maker gives everyone gifts. Though they are not all the same, we each play an important role in the great song. None is more important than another.'

Delvina shook her head. How could that be? What was so special about her? How could she compare to these graceful people? 'Why does he stay on the prow like that, though?' Perhaps to feel the wind and spray.

'Watching, listening, sensing, learning—the song of the waves, the wind and the life-pulse of creatures in this place. Only by knowing a form inside out can we change into it. Korak's son is keen to learn a multitude of forms before, perhaps, he masters the ones he already knows. Always in such a rush, but then he is young.'

'Is there a limit to how many creatures you can change into?'

'No, not really, though most learn three or four—' Highwun Bikan's eyes narrowed and she stopped speaking.

The Mariner's daughter, Ariel, strode across the deck towards them with a practised rolling stride, her long honey-brown hair and sleeveless robe flapping in the wind. She glanced toward Zadeki, a dreamy look in her face, before continuing to walk towards Highwun Bikan and Delvina. No doubt, Ariel would be a better match for a young shapeshifter. Delvina squashed the thought.

'Daughter of Habbiah,' Highwun Bikan said.

'Shapeshifter. My father asks you to fulfil your agreement. You know what you're looking for?'

'I do.' With a wry smile, Bikan handed the cup to Ariel. She walked with a lithe grace towards Zadeki and touched his shoulder. 'Come with me, son of Korak.'

Running along the deck, she leapt into the air, effortlessly turning into a seabird with wide wingspan like the one in Delvina's dreams.

'Yay!' Zadeki lept to his feet and followed. Changing into the form of a sea eagle, he swooped over the white-capped waves before shadowing Highwun Bikan's climb into the white-blue sky.

Ariel inhaled sharply. 'Then it is true, they can transform. I thought it a tale for younglings.' She turned back to Delvina. 'I don't suppose you do that?'

Delvina shook her head. If only she could, then she wouldn't be left behind in so many ways.

Retza shovelled the last load of rubble into the heaped-up glimmer truck and stood back to the side of the tunnel. Watcher Manoah whistled the all clear. The truck jerked and reversed back down the track toward the staging area and the allure of crib comforts. Retza rubbed the sweat rolling down his brow. It was steamy in here and he was exhausted, but they'd only completed half a shift. Glimmer lights had been re-installed along the walls and the ventilation fans were working overtime to filter the dust and keep the air fresh.

'Take a break,' Yalom, Lead Hand of Diamond North, called out.

'About time,' Stone Singer Peta muttered under her breath.

Retza blew on his blistered palms and slid down the tunnel wall, ignoring the dampness.

Manoah sauntered up and tossed him a ration pack. 'You know you're a watcher now and don't need to do this grunt work.'

Retza waved a hand at him, too tired to argue or explain his need to help in the search for his former crib mates.

He pulled down the scarf wrapped around his mouth and nose and took a bite of the dried sava root biscuit. It wasn't a taste he was used to, but it was food at least.

'Uggh, this abovegrounder food,' one of the crew griped.

'Stop whining, it's food isn't it?' Peta said.

'We shouldn't be building the tunnel to Outside,' someone further down the tunnel said. 'The Dark Ones forbade it.'

'Who said that?' Lead Hand Yalom demanded, but no one responded.

Secondwun Nebam stood staring at the blocked tunnel, his jaw clenching and unclenching, his eyes haunted. Havilah had finally given a deadline on the rescue efforts.

Somewhere in the distance, water trickled onto rock. With each passing heartbeat, the chances of finding any of the Greenstone South crew were melting away. Not that it had ever been great, but until they found the bodies, hope could still cling on to the tiniest foothold.

A soft hum and the tik tak tik tak of metal wheels on rails announced the return of the glimmer trucks loaded with supports. A glimmer-powered digger with clawed scoop sat squat and ominous on the flatbed of the first truck.

Despair weighted down Retza's limbs and stole his appetite. The time for less cautious measures had come.

Lead Hand Yalom swallowed the last bite and slugged his water. With a groan, he stood up and walked over to Nebam.

'Time to make the hard decisions, Secondwun. If we don't get the tunnel through in time, we could all die,' he said in a low voice.

Nebam rubbed his red-rimmed eyes with dust-stained fingers. 'Do your worst,' he growled.

Retza looked down and blinked the grit from his eyes. The Greenstone South crew were out of time.

Yalom put two fingers in his mouth and whistled. 'Listen up! Clear the tracks and bring the digger forward. And the rest of you lot, bring in the supports.'

Over the next few hours, the digger bit into the piled debris, tossing its load into trucks. Retza and Manoah stayed close to Nebam, keeping an eye on proceedings. The rest of the crew worked at keeping the tracks clear and shoring up the tunnel as they went.

Retza felt cold seeping into his boots. He glanced down. A dark shadow crept across the floor, reflecting the line of rigged glimmer lights and foaming around the bigger obstructions. Like water. His heart rammed into his ribs.

'Stop the digger,' he yelled, pitching his voice above the crunching of rocks and whine of the machine. He raced toward the end of the tunnel. 'Stop, stop, stop!'

'What?' Yalom turned toward him, wiping his forehead.

'Get back down the tunnel. Water's coming from the other side.'

The rubble wall blocking the tunnel bulged like a

sponge sucking up liquid. Water trickled through tiny gaps and holes.

'By the pit, in the trucks! Now!' Yalom yelled, scrambling backwards.

Toolwuns raced to the empty trucks at the back.

Nebam stayed, standing legs apart, staring at the bulging wall.

'Come on, Secondwun,' Retza called. But he didn't move.

Pushing against the now ankle-deep water, Retza grabbed Nebam's arm, pulling him back toward the glimmer trucks.

'Do you need a hand?' Lead Hand Yalom yelled.

'Go ahead, sir. I'm closer,' Peta turned back, wading through the churning flood.

Rocks and spray tumbled forward. The digger sputtered and died.

'We have to go,' Manoah yelled. 'Before it kills the power to the glimmer trucks."

Yalom jumped on a coupling. 'Come on!'

'I can't wait any longer.' Manoah pulled the switch and jumped inside as the trucks rocked and shuddered. Slow at first.

The water swirled higher, threatening to pull Retza's feet from under him. There was still time to catch up if they moved. He grabbed Nebam's arm. Peta reached out to grab the other side.

The trucks jerked backwards down the tunnel, first slow, then faster, leaving them behind.

With a sudden strange whoosh, the wall of rubble burst open like an overripe fruit. A wash of foam and water and rocks rushed towards them. The digger slid backwards along the newly cleared tracks, tilting to the side.

A rock crashed into Nebam and he fell forward. All three tumbled together in the cold, foaming water. Nebam slipped from his fingers. Retza thrashed about, pushing his head above the churning water, coughing. He half crawled half paddled toward the digger, now on its side and jammed against the wall. The water rushed in torrents pushing him.

With a phuft, the lights fizzed out, abandoning Retza to the deep dark void.

The ship pitched, crashing Danel into the wall of the hold. The small breakfast he'd risked this morning, climbed up his throat. He clutched his stomach and swallowed it down.

Bad decision. He should have stayed above decks, but his eyes ached at the endless horizon, the dizzying open sky, with its grey threat of rain. What in Nardva was he doing here, in a flimsy wooden vessel perched on the contrary surface of this massive body of water? At any moment, a wave might sweep them all into the fathoms deep and he would sink like a counterweight to the bottom, if it had one. Even if he survived, what did he have to say to these silver-skinned giants. Adelphi, Vaane, they all looked the same to him.

A long corridor ran the length of the ship with doors off either side—accommodations for the crew, rooms to store cargo, a place to prepare and cook food. Some of the ship's crew pushed past him, hastily averting their eyes when he returned their stares. Unlike the Forest Folk or indeed the Harbour Master, Warden, or Mariner, most had rust to clay-coloured skins and were closer to him in height.

Another one pushed past, intent on some errand.

'Hey, can you tell me which way ...'

But she was gone with barely a glance. The ship beneath him heaved and he staggered backward. His foot found empty space. His heart shuddered and shock zipped through his muscles.

'Blast it.'

He flung out his arms, trying to grab hold of something, anything. No railing, no objects, nothing. He banged his way down the hatchway ladder and landed on the tilted floor, as battered as a rock in a crushing barrel.

The boards vibrated beneath him and the sharp ozone smell tingled the close air. After a moment, he sat up, groaning at the throbbing all over. He rubbed his shoulders and hip and shins. At least, nothing seemed broken.

A soft aquamarine glow cast shadows on the walls, a light similar to the glimmer lights at home. It came from an open doorway.

'About time you got here.' A bulky figure, that reminded him of Gilarth, stepped into the doorway, blocking the light and throwing Danel into shadow.

'But ...'

'Get in here now!' The man disappeared back into the room.

Danel pulled himself up and stumbled toward the door, drawn by the light. Was this the Sea Heart the sailors referred to? It couldn't hurt to have a look and maybe take his mind off the lurching of the ship.

He entered a long, low room, the white wood of the ship's hull forming both sides. At the centre was an array of greenish crystals set in a brass console, similar to the Crystal Heart but smaller. The console was connected to a long vertical rod penetrating the roof. Another spinning horizontal rod ran along to the end of the ship. A soft hum and static surrounded him.

The large worker turned, his rust-coloured eyes narrowing. His hair was white, his face weathered. 'What? You're not crew. What are you doing here?'

Danel stood taller. 'I'm looking for the storeroom.'

'Bit lost, aren't you?' The man peered at a dial, then spun a knob. 'Since you are here, make yourself useful. Bring me a wrench.'

Danel rubbed his skinned knuckles on his breeches and looked around. 'Where ...?'

'Over there.'

The tool cabinet was built in against the curved wall of the hull. Danel took down the wrench and handed it to the ebed. 'Is there a problem?'

'Temperamental, she is. She's not been in service for many years, because her crystals are depleted and her hull old and weathered, not unlike me.' He spun, loosened a knob and tinkered inside reminiscent of Scrybe Barekia.

'Are you a techwun?' Danel asked. 'How does it work?'

The man nodded, his eyes still fixed on the dials. 'Yeah. Name's Jonan.' He ran a loving hand over the brass panel. 'Works like most soul-bound crystals—in this case the Sea Heart captures and expands the vibrations from the wind and waves and transmits it to a shaft which can push us along when the wind fails us.'

'Fascinating.' Sounded like the Crystal Heart. Danel grabbed onto the back of the console to steady himself against the sudden movement of the ship.

'So who are you? You're not from Redhaven, that's for sure.'

'I'm a toolwun or was until Havilah became Overseer. Now I'm Speaker and Thirdwun Danel.'

'Speaker, huh? The scuttlebutt is, you come from the Sea Dragon King's mines in the White Mountains.'

Danel thrust out his chin. 'Our mines now. We dug them, we maintain them, we work them and without outsider help.' Well, up until now, but he wasn't going to admit more than he had to. 'Is the Sea Stone soul-bound to you then?'

'Nah, not to an ebed like me. To the Mariner and his line. Which is why Warden Ealam pressured him to help.' Jonan gave him a hard look. 'Bit nosey aren't you.' He rubbed his chin and dropped his voice. 'To be honest, there are some that say you lot had the right idea of it ... going it alone. But be careful in Silantis. The council will use you and discard you like a seaberry pip. And watch out for those shapeshifters. A man would be a fool to trust them. Don't trust any of those silverskins. A nest of sea snakes and kraken, if you ask me.'

Danel's stomach squirmed. 'The Forest Folk have helped us.'

'So what do they want?' Techwun Jonan flicked his hands. 'You better get. If Mariner Habbiah finds you down here, you'll have a whole lot of explaining to do. Go back up the ladder and turn right—you'll find the storerooms in the bow.' He winked. 'Maybe we'll meet again, if you survive Silantis that is.'

Danel ducked his head and made for the door—his nausea increased by a sudden sense of unease. Would he ever again feel the solid stone of the Caverns beneath his feet?

Grey clouds scudded on the eastern horizon, the restless waters beneath turning a slate grey, tipped with the occasional white cap. Zadeki dipped his wings and used his second transparent eyelids to shield his eyes against the buffeting of the wind, one of the advantages of being a bird. His powerful pectorals strained against the sudden air gusts. After the forays with Aunt Bikan or Baba, he was beginning to get the feel for the new flying conditions.

'The direction of the currents is different here.' Aunt Bikan's feathers ruffled along her long wingspan as the wind strengthened.

He tilted his head, sharp sea-eagle eyes scanning the pattern made as the long rolling waves intercepted each other. He hit an air pocket, dropped a couple of tanis, and pushed down with his wings to regain height. He needed to work harder in his sea-eagle form than Aunt Bikan with her albatross form.

A strange smell tickled his nostril holes and he opened his beak, tilting from side to side, to taste the wind. Salt and seaweed and something else, resinous ... coming in gusts from the northwest.

'Tree sap ...' Aunt Bikan said. 'Can you smell it?'

'Yes.' Though this wasn't as sharp as mountain pine or as rich as the trees of the Forest, it was something similar. 'To the right.'

He banked, honing in the direction of the strongest smell. White flecks swirled against the grey horizon like large, wet snowflakes.

'Birds,' he said.

'A flock of seagulls,' Aunt Bikan said at the same time.

They looked at one another and keened a laugh. Going on sweeps with Da-Baba's sister wasn't as painful as he feared it would be. She actually knew a thing or two and was happy to teach him.

'Do you think it is the island?' he asked.

'Could be another ship. Either way, we should check it out.'

He nodded and followed as she changed course. Soon the smudge of land appeared on the horizon, and with it the low roar of the surf. The first island they flew over, was small, with wiry tufts of grass and stunted bushes ringed with a shallow underwater shelf.

'Coral reef,' Aunt Bikan keened. 'This looks promising.' She turned further north.

A trail of small, round islands led like an ant trail to a bigger humpedbacked island with three conical peaks cloaked in dense green vegetation. A smaller island snuggled against its flank like a whale calf close to its mother.

Standing sentinel above the small island's stark cliffs, a tower, a twin of the one in Redhaven, speared up into the turbid air. The circular glass face on its top was shattered and soot stained the white stones and blackened the conical roof. A frisson of fear ran through Zadeki. Surely that wasn't normal.

'Sentinel Isle and, across the strait on the big island, Safety Bay and White Haven. Stay close and shield your thoughts if you can.'

The waves rolled in unconcerned by petty bipedal affairs, curling into foamed-edged peaks and windswept manes before dashing themselves against the tall cliffs in a mass of white spray. Seabirds—gulls, terns, and albatross—swirled around in a cacophony of sound.

'I can't see the harbour.' Zadeki's words were whipped away by the wind, but Aunt Bikan tipped her wing toward the north in answer.

Past the Sentinel Island, he saw an opening in the dark-grey cliffs of the bigger island, another smaller tower on one side, leading into a circular bay.

'Fly high,' Bikan keened. 'Keep out of arrow range.'

A shudder shook Zadeki. Would the Vaane really shoot them down? After their cool reception at Redhaven, it seemed possible.

They flew over the heads of the enclosed bay and looked down on devastation.

White ships—sails shredded, wooden sides splintered—lay piled into a makeshift barrier across the entrance. On the land, smoke rose from many of the buildings and further back, figures crouched behind barricades across the streets made of carts and furniture. Beyond that armed watchers stood behind rough earthen walls with great wooden machines standing like confused giants.

'Invaders?' Zadeki asked. But who could they be? They were too far south, and it had been far too many centuries for the wars in the north to have reached them now.

Bikan waggled her wings. 'I see only Vaane ships. It could be an internal conflict. We need to report to the Mariner.' She looped around, flying over the pincers of land enclosing the bay.

They flew back towards the White Rose in silence. Zadeki traced the magnetic fields against the angle of the sun and the pattern of the waves.

In the east the clouds piled on top of one other, white tops reflecting the sun's brilliance but darkened and bruised underneath. Moments later, the small patch of white bobbed against the great expanse of grey-green. Aunt Bikan flew to their goal with unerring accuracy.

Bikan landed first, transforming into her human

form with smooth practice. Zadeki followed, slamming into the deck as it pitched upward. He tumbled and scraped his shins.

Delvina rushed up. She lurched to the side and grabbed on to Danel to keep her balance. Baba joined them.

'Are you alright?' she huffed.

Zadeki sighed ruefully. 'Sure. Just lost a bit of skin.' The waves towered higher than before, tilting the ship as it climbed up the waves.

Aunt Bikan pulled her tari around her sparse form, not bothering to chide him for his clumsiness. 'Where is Mariner Habbiah, brother's-son,' she asked tersely.

'In the chart room.' Baba stretched out a hand and pulled Zadeki up. 'Big storm's coming from the east.'

As though to confirm Baba's words, the ship dipped down and a rush of waves sloshed over the deck. The Mariner and Ariel emerged from below decks. Mariner Habbiah beckoned them over. 'Did you find land?'

'Yes, we did, about five lek to the north-west. We can lead you there, but there is something else you need to know. The harbour is barricaded, the ships wrecked and there is fighting in White Haven.'

The Captain frowned. 'Can the White Rose get through?

'Ship wreckage is strewn from one end of the bay to the other,' Zadeki said.

'And armed parties contesting the area. Son of the Sea, is there another place to land on the Main Island?'

Ariel pressed her hands to her side. 'The harbour is the only shelter for a ship this size. Most of the island is hemmed in by steep cliffs. No beaches to land on.' Ariel turned to her father. 'Should we turn back, Baba?'

'Not with the storm on our tail.'

The ship shuddered beneath Zadeki's feet. So small and fragile a protection in the maw of the waves.

'Then what can you do?' Danel asked, grey-faced and white-eyed.

'Ride the storm.' The Mariner said grimly. 'Unless ... Shapeshifter Bikan, can you detect rocks beneath the waves with those sharp bird senses?'

Aunt Bikan and Baba looked at each other, then Aunt Bikan nodded once. 'It's possible, but that won't help us get into Safe Harbour.'

'Destruction Bay is another further round the Main Island to the south.'

That didn't sound so good.

Ariel sucked in air. 'The White Rose is too big to survive the Grinder even with a pilot, Baba.'

Understanding dawned. 'But we can fly ahead, alert you of hidden rocks,' Zadeki said.

'In these conditions,' Aunt Bikan shook her head. 'Difficult and dangerous.'

The Mariner's daughter brushed his arm. 'Please, it may be our only hope.'

A squall of horizontal rain slammed into them, soaking Zadeki's already damp sarum. He shivered. The waves reared up about them like turbulent, sliding hills. Delvina and Danel had no way to get off the ship.

'Let's do it,' Delvina said, her chin trembling 'We haven't come all this way to drown. We've got a mission to complete.'

Mariner Habbiah struck his palm with his fist. 'We'll do it, but we have to get to the bay first. Zadeki you're with me, you other two be ready to fly ahead at my command.'

Danel moved closer to Delvina. 'What can we do to help?'

'You? Get down below and keep out of the way.' The Mariner turned and cupped his hand to his mouth and yelled. 'Second, reef the sails, all but the try-sail. I'll take the wheel. Inform Techwun Jonan, I'll need full crystal power.'

Zadeki hastened after the Mariner and Ariel into the teeth of the wind.

'Secondwun Nebam? Peta?' Retza called out into the heavy dense darkness, his voice bouncing back at him from the sides of a much larger cavern than he'd been in moments before. He clung to the wheels of the digger and pulled himself up the side, out of the power of the swirling water sucking at his legs. Small waves and rocks bashed against the side of the tunnel with a wet, slapping sound.

'Nebam?' He called again. If he stayed on the digger, someone would eventually come back for him. He hoped.

'Retza, I've got Nebam,' a voice spluttered in the darkness.

'Peta! Follow my voice. There's room here on the digger.' Retza pulled out his truncheon and strained his eyes against the coal-black darkness in the direction of the toolwun.

Splashing came from the left, closer and closer. A low groan.

'Grab my truncheon,' Retza called out.

A surge of sound and the truncheon pulled down. Hooking his leg behind a clawed scoop, he reached out and grabbed a jerkin and pulled. With a couple of grunts and yelps, Peta clambered up beside him.

'Here, help with Secondwun Nebam.'

Together they reefed him in. The digger tilted.

'Quick, move further back.' The last thing they needed was to be tipped back into the water. They scrunched against the wall. Retza counted the seconds. The digger trembled then settled. Retza's heartbeat slowed to a more normal rhythm and his limbs went wobbly. For now, they were safe. All they had to do was wait for rescue.

'Why so much water?' Retza wondered.

'Underground river,' Nebam croaked.

Of course, Retza berated himself. Either a misplaced charge or the cave-in must have made an opening into one of the underground waterways. Only the large pile of rubble from the roof-fall had prevented it from flowing further down the tunnel. The first rapid flow of water could even have undermined the stability of the tunnel supports. He shuddered. Hopefully more roof wouldn't soon follow.

'Are you alright, Secondwun?' Peta asked.

Nebam grunted. 'Might have hit my head. Did the others get out?'

'Yes, I think so,' Retza said, the image of the trucks disappearing down the tunnel engraved on his mind. But perhaps Manoah had done the right thing.

'Retza, unfasten the glimmer torch on my belt. My blasted arm's not working.'

'Will water have got in?' asked Peta.

'Won't find out until we switch it on, will we.'

Retza untied the torch, rubbing it against the dry leather of his watcher jacket, and pressed the switch. A beam of blue-white light flashed out across the dark, restless water and burned an afterimage in his eyes.

Instead of being piled up with rubble, the tunnel opened out into a large cavern filled with an underground lake. Small waves lapped up against the walls and continued to swirl past them, covering the glimmer truck tracks and reaching over halfway up the walls. Smaller rocks still bumped against each other in the flow. Probably too deep to wade out, at least until the force of the flood calmed down some more. Retza hoped it didn't go too far up the tunnel. One thing he did know. He couldn't swim.

He flashed the light back to the black lake that stretched out further than the torchlight could reach. Crystals covered the roof, flashing the light back in rainbow colours.

'Beautiful,' Peta said.

'Aye, you could say that. But there will be no tunnelling through that.' Nebam hugged his ribs with one arm, the other hanging at an awkward angle. His hair was matted with blood on one side.

The air went out of Retza's lungs. The Secondwun was right. They could bring down pumps, but they'd be unlikely to cope with this amount of water. Not in time. And there wasn't time to start another tunnel either.

Maybe it would have been better to have drowned than face the slow starvation.

'Don't be silly,' Delvina's voice seemed as real as if she was beside him. He remembered her face on the journey across the mountains, cold, grey, sun and wind burned, hungry and stubborn. She wouldn't give up and neither would he.

'Hello,' a faint voice echoed across the water.

'Who's there?' Retza shone the torch up the tunnel but nothing had changed.

'Hello,' the voice came again, soft and shaking.

'It's from the cavern,' Peta said, her eyes like dark tunnels. 'Do you think it's the Dark Ones?'

Nebam pulled himself up, a puzzled frown on his narrow face. 'I know that voice.' He blinked and gripped his head with both hands.

Retza's hand shook. He did too. 'Karel,' he whispered.

'Secondwun of Greenstone South,' Peta said.

Were they hearing the spirits of those who died in the cave-in—or the survivors?

'Can you help us?'

Nebam cupped his hand around his mouth and leaned out. 'Secondwun Karel, who's with you?'

'There's … eighteen of us. But we're in a bad way. Can you help us.'

Nebam, Peta and Retza exchanged looks. They were survivors, not ghosts.

'Help is coming,' Nebam called out. 'Help is coming.'

Cold seawater ran along the wooden floor and sloshed against Delvina's boots. Outside, thunder rumbled, the waves roared, and the wind moaned and howled. A low vibrating hum, more felt than heard, came from the floor below them.

Delvina shivered, her fingers numb from gripping the framework. 'It's worse not knowing what's happening above decks.' The rising nausea and the feeling of being helpless, like a baby bat caught in the current of an underground torrent, threatened to overwhelm her. Had they reached Destruction Bay yet? It seemed like a full shift had passed by, though it was perhaps only hours since they'd been ordered below deck.

Danel nodded, his face a pale blur in the dim light. 'The Mariner knows what to do and the Forest Folk are helping.'

A bone-jarring thud, and the sides of the hull shivered.

Danel started, then growled. 'Maybe I should find out what's happening.'

'I'm coming too.'

If she was going to die, she'd rather die in the open, though she'd never thought she'd think such a thing. But this was no cavern and the wooden walls seemed as thin as a cave swallow's eggshell, fragile protection between her and drowning. Besides, she worried about Zadeki and the others battling against the winds and waves outside.

Holding on to each other, they staggered along the heaving storeroom, toward the corridor and the stairs to the deck above. Danel pulled her through the doorway, his grip strong and reassuring.

'Hey, you, where are you going?' a voice boomed out from behind them. A curly head poked up from the access to the lower hull.

'Going up,' Danel grunted.

'You mad? You'll be swept into the sea at the first contrary wave. Besides, Techwun Jonan needs extra hands down here. Come on.' The ebed waved them down and disappeared.

Delvina looked at Danel then glanced at the hatchway to the deck. Going deeper into the belly of the ship seemed a mad idea.

'We should help if we can,' Danel said.

She took a big breath of salt-heavy air. 'Alright.'

They turned and staggered back the way they'd come, then half climbed, half fell down the ladder. Ankle-high waves of water slapped into them, tugging at their feet.

'Careful.' Danel led her to a doorway.

He pushed the door open. The ship bucked and tilted. Danel gripped the doorframe and Delvina grabbed hold of his waist.

Pulsating blue-green light lit up the room and reflected off the swirling water, sending interlacing dancing beams across the low roof. In the centre, ebed crew piled sandbags around a smaller version of the Crystal Heart.

The man studying the dials at the panel looked up. 'Don't stand there. Danel, help Remon here with caulking the leak. If the Sea Stone gets drenched, we'll be swimming with the fishes.'

'Aye, Techwun Jonan.' Danel waded toward the indicated worker and Delvina followed.

'Hey you, what's your name?'

'Delvina.'

'Right, well get topside and take this message to the Mariner. With the force of the storm on the hull, we're springing more leaks than a baby. He needs to engage the secondary sea-pumps.'

Delvina blinked. 'Me?'

'Yeah, you. Everyone else is busy. Now go.'

With a last trailing glance at Danel, Delvina retraced her steps.

She struggled up the stairs and cracked open the hatchway. Water gushed in drenching her and threatening to prise loose her grip. She clung to the railing and, past shivering, pulled herself onto the tilting deck and slammed the hatch shut. Wind and rain slashed into her eyes.

All about her was confusion, sheets of rain thrashing

her in stinging icy blows, wind tugging and pulling at hair and clothes and limbs, the sky rolling and rocking, the deck bucking beneath her feet. Nothing had ever prepared her for this.

The sails were furled and tied on the masts, even the triangular storm sail. Mariner Habbiah stood at the tiller at the stern, legs wide and rolling with the erratic movements of the deck. His daughter beside him, one hand on her crystal. Two albatrosses hovered at the bow of the ship, feathers ruffled. The slanting rain eased, and, for a spine-tingling moment, steep sharp-edged cliffs loomed out of the mist in front of the ship.

Delvina turned her back on the harrowing sight. She gripped a guide rope and bent her head into the wind and driving rain, staggering toward the Mariner. She couldn't see Zadeki.

A wave crested over the side, crashing on the deck and flooding over her. Maker help her, she couldn't hold on much longer. Maker help them all.

Her feet slipped. Strong hands caught her and pulled her to her feet. The water ebbed away, leaving her weak-legged and shaking.

'Del, you should be below deck.' Zadeki shouted in her ear, his voice hard to hear above the bone-shaking scream of wind and waves. His hair was flattened to his face.

She looked away. 'I have a message for the Mariner from the Techwun Jonan.'

'Give it to me. You need to get below,'

'Techwun Jonan says, 'The Hull is leaking too much. The Mariner should engage the secondary sea-pumps.''

Lightning lit up the battered sky in a searing flash.

'Got it. Now get below, Del, it's too dangerous on deck.'

Zadeki ran toward the Captain, seeming to anticipate each uncertain move of the ship. His soaked sarum clung to his muscular legs and torso. Delvina blinked the water out of her eyes, her heart pounding. One wave and surely he would be swept away.

When he reached the stern. Ariel turned, and he leant in close, speaking into her ear. She nodded and tugged her father's coat. Mariner Habbiah cupped his hands and bellowed, though his words came to Delvina in snatches.

She shook herself. Zadeki was right, she needed to get below.

The shuddering in the ship eased for a heartbeat. Keeping a grip on the soggy rope, Delvina turned back toward the hatchway. The deck dropped beneath her feet as the prow dipped down, ploughing a furrow through the churning white foam between two jagged rock walls. Her heart rammed against her spine, stealing her breath away.

Was this the Grinder? Whatever it was, they were going in.

The prow lifted out of the maelstrom, water streaming past both sides and down the deck. The two albatrosses wheeled ahead, swooping dangerously close to the churning foam, guiding the ship. And just beyond the white, a glimpse of calmer waters in a wide, enclosed bay.

A sudden lull in the wind and rain, as though the storm was taking a breath, and the fury of the waves dampened. Grey walls slid past so close she could almost touch them.

Her breath puffed out in a soft mist. They were going to make it. After ten long days since leaving Tarka, she would stand beside Danel and face down the Sea Dragon King and fight for the fate of her people.

'Delvina, watch out.' Zadeki's voice carried in the strange stillness.

Hand on the guide rope, she twisted round and her muscles clenched tight. A massive wave, grey-green and laced with foam, towered over the stern, rising higher and higher.

Move! Move! Move!

But she couldn't.

The tip of the wave curled over, the sides rebounding against the rock walls in white fury. Slowly, the edge curled and rolled and fell—down, down, down—onto the White Rose, slamming into the deck. The mast screeched and shattered. Water rammed into Delvina, pushing her tumbling along the deck and against the railing. She grabbed, clutched, dug her feet in. Her fingers slipped.

She fell, water all around her.

The seawater hit her like a rockfall. She couldn't breathe. Dark-green water surrounded her, white bubbles streamed from her nose, water rushed in her ears, muting the renewed roar of the storm.

She struggled to find the sky, her heart pounding, her lungs burning, but she couldn't. She had to breathe. Water everywhere, so much water.

A sudden roaring in her ears. Her face slapped with cold wind, head above water. She gulped air and seawater, coughing, salt burning her nose and throat.

Through blurred eyes, she saw the ship ahead of her, like a broken white bird.

'Here, I'm here.'

Another wave doused her, pushing her down. A strong current tugged at her. Her breath escaped in silver bubbles, like diamonds, like tears. She reached out a hand to catch them.

Darkness fringed her vision, stars sparkled in the dark edges. She needed to take another breath. She was going to die. She'd failed her mission.

Help, please help us.

She stopped struggling, a warm peace enfolding her. She didn't need to be a hero. She hoped that Danel would survive and find the secret of the gate. Zadeki and the Forest Folk would help him. Her only regret, that she didn't say goodbye to Retza.

The darkness deepened, swirling around her. Her thoughts frayed, and she let go the struggle, sinking like a stone to its resting place.

Strong arms surrounded her. A silver angel. She hugged the vision tight. Hard muscles beneath the silvery-luminous skin, pulled her upward, above the churning waves.

The peace shattered, and pain washed over her. She coughed, water flowing from her mouth and nose. She took another shuddering, burning breath and struggled.

'Relax, let me take you.' Zadeki's hoarse voice tickled her ear.

A cold wind stung her cheeks and her salt-rimmed eyes. Something scratched her skin beneath her. Someone or something dragged her, then she was still. Shallow waves washed over her.

After a while, she pushed herself onto hands and knees, pushed the hair out of her eyes.

Zadeki lay beside her gasping. The water sucked back from under them, slicing furrows in the grey sand. Another wave, with foaming white caps rushed towards them. She grabbed Zadeki and with her last remaining strength, pulled them both further up, towards the steep cliffs. After a moment, he groaned, rolled over and got up on hands and knees and crawled with her. Together, shivering and exhausted, they huddled at the base of the cliff.

'The ship.' Zadeki croaked.

Delvina sat up and rubbed the brine from her eyes with wrinkled fingers.

The clouds parted in a bloody sky to show the White Rose riding on the waves, one mast half broken off. Two albatrosses flew in ever wider circles, their mournful keening travelling across the white-capped water.

'It's intact, more or less.' A bubble of hope rose in her chest. Maybe, Danel and the other survived. She turned to the Zadeki. 'You saved my life. You almost died doing it.'

Zadeki pushed back the bedraggled hair from his face. 'I couldn't let you drown. Retza would kill me.' He hugged her tight.

She hugged him back, her spirits soaring.

'Zadeki, I love you.' She blurted. Shocked at her blunt words, but it was true. She did. Maybe from the first time she'd seen him, protesting Retza's plan to eat him.

He patted her back. 'I know. You and Retza are like sister and brother to me.'

'That's .... I mean ... '

He didn't see her like that. Of course, he didn't. A stumpy, toolwun, so unlike the Mariner's daughter. She'd known that and been foolish enough to hope. Tears welled on her lashes and rolled down salt-rimmed cheeks.

'Hey, Delvina, it's going to be alright. We're here, we've made it to the Lonely Isles and with courage like yours, the Vaane will not dare deny you the answers you need.' Zadeki squeezed her hand.

Delvina swallowed her tears and smiled. Her heart

was breaking, but that wasn't important right now. She'd been chasing a fool's dream while her people were slowly starving. They needed the seal. They needed answers. They needed her to be strong.

She stuffed down her treacherous emotions, refusing to listen to them. Whatever it took, she'd get the answers for them. Until that was done, and she returned home to Retza, her journey was incomplete.

TO BE CONTINUED

The sequel, Shadow Crystals, is now available March 2019.

Author Note

If you've enjoyed this story from the world of Nardva, please leave a fair and honest review on Amazon, Goodreads and/or your favourite reviewing site. Writing reviews (no matter how short), helps support authors to keep on creating and publishing the stories you enjoy.

Want to keep up to date with new releases, giveaways and events? Sign up for my email newsletter Jeanette O'Hagan Writes http://eepurl.com/bbLJKT

You might also like:

Heart of the Mountain–first novella in Under the Mountain series
Blood Crystal–second novella in Under the Mountain series
Shadow Crystals–fourth novella in Under the Mountain series
Akrad's Children–the first in the Akrad's Legacy series
Ruhanna's Flight and other stories—a collection of short stories, mostly set in Nardva

Coming Soon
Caverns of the Deep–book 5 in the Under the Mountain series
Rasel's Song–book 2 in the Akrad's Legacy series –2019
Chameleon Protocols trilogy 2018/2019.

Character List

Adrilla (Kupanna of the Tamrin)
Ariel (The Mariner's daughter)
Barekia (Scrybe, Putarn & Nebam's grandmother)
Bikan (Elder & daughter of Kinleader Telsima)
Danel (Thirdwun of Darane, Havilah's nephew)
Delvina (Messenger of Darane, Retza's twin sister)
Ealam (Warden of Redhaven)
Gilarth (Head Watcher of the Darane)
Gregan (Farm Lead Hand)
Habbiah (Mariner of the Vaane)
Havilah (New Overseer, Putarn & Nebam's mother)
Hezikah (the old Overseer Uzza's father)
Jasalim (Pathfinder of the Kin, Telsima's son)
Jesson (son of Uzza, Zara's younger brother)
Karel, (Secondwun of the Greenstone South Crew)
Korak (Pathfinder, Zadeki's baba)
Manoah (Watcher, Darane)
Nakrin (Madomo of the Tamrin)
Narval (Darane Quartermaster)
Nebam (Secondwun and son of Havilah)
Peta (Stone/Rock singer of Copper East)
Putarn (son of Havilah)
Rebekka (Harbour Master at Redhaven)
Retza (Watcher of Darane, twin brother of Delvina)
Supak (Kapok of Tamrin, Adrilla's son)
Telsima (Kinleader of Forest Folk or Kin)
Timon (Secondwun of the Watchers)
Uzza (old Overseer deposed by Havilah)
Wulapa (Kapok, Supak Kapok's father)
Zadeki (Jazadek, Korak's son)
Zara (daughter of the Old Overseer)

Acknowledgements

Stone of the Sea is the third novella in the Under the Mountain series. It is not the last, with another two books planned, *Shadow Crystals* and *Caverns of the Deep*. When I first started to write a short story based on the theme 'glimpses of light', I had no idea how far it would carry me. From delving deep into the dark corners of a mining realm, to the edges of the Great Forest of the Forest Folk, and even across the ocean to the Lonely Isles. These places were already a reality from plotting and daydreaming the Akrad's Legacy series (of which only Akrad's Children has so far been published), but it has been exhilarating to explore them in greater detail and in a different time period. And Delvina, Retza and Zadeki have wormed their way into my heart.

Writing isn't a solitary pastime. I am especially grateful to my critique-partners, beta-readers, editors and proof readers who have helped me polish and refine my work. So many people and places have been an inspiration for my world building, from the mines of Mt Isa to a couple of voyages across the Indian Ocean, to rainforests of my homeland, among books and movies and other research.

Special thanks to my sister Kathleen Hillenberg who is such an enthusiastic and untiring supporter and has given great feedback on practically every story I've written. Also Suzanne Hay-Bartlem, Nola Passmore, Lynne Stringer, Raelene Purtill, Adam Collings, Cate McKeown, Linsey Painter and Neasa Nic Dhómhnaill.

Nola Passmore of The Write Flourish is a fantastic editor and I love her work.

I'm grateful for my family—my loving husband Tony, my precious children Kathleen and David, my parents Tom and Jean Curtis—who instilled in me a love of faith and fantasy—and siblings, Tom Curtis, Frank Curtis, Chris Curtis and Kathleen Hillenberg, with whom I've shared many wonderful adventures.

Most of all, I'm grateful to my Maker in whose creative footsteps I can only hope to follow.

Jeanette O'Hagan 27 October 2018

About the Author

Jeanette O'Hagan enjoys writing fiction, poetry, blogging and editing. She is writing her Akrad's Legacy Series—a Young Adult secondary world fantasy fiction with adventure, courtly intrigue and romantic elements. Her short stories and poems are published in a number of anthologies including The Quantum Soul, Tales From the Underground, Futurevision and Glimpses of Light. She has published now four novellas in the Under the Mountain series, her debut novel Akrad's Children and a collection of short stories, Ruhanna's Flight and other stories.

Jeanette has practised medicine, studied communication, history, theology and, more recently, a Master's in writing. She is a member of a number of writers' groups. She loves reading, painting, travel, catching up for coffee with friends and pondering the meaning of life. Jeanette lives in Brisbane with her husband and children.

Check out the social media of your choice—though Jeanette is most active on *Facebook, Twitter, GoodReads, Pinterest* and *Instagram*—and *Amazon Central* has all her books in one place.

Links and updates can be found at her website *Jeanette O'Hagan Writes* http://jeanetteohagan.com or her email newsletter http://eepurl.com/bbLJKT

Other Publications

Novels

Akrad's Legacy series
Akrad's Children (By the Light Books, 2017)
Rasel's Song – due 2019
Mannok's Betrayal – due 2019

Novellas

Under the Mountain series:
Heart of the Mountain: a short novella (By the Light Books, 2016)
Blood Crystal: a novella (By the Light Books, 2017)
Stone of the Sea: a novella – (By the Light Books, 2018)
Shadow Crystals: a novella – (By the Light Books, 2019)
Caverns of the Deep: a novella — due May/June 2019

Short Stories:

Tales of the South:
Ruhanna's Flight and other stories, (By the Light Books, 2018)
'Shadows of the Deep' in Tales From the Underground, (Inklings Press, 2017)
'The Herbalist's Daughter' (By the Light Books, 2016; originally in Tied in Pink romance anthology, (Far Horizons, 2014)
'Lakwi's Lament' (By the Light Books, 2017) originally in Like a Girl Plan anthology, (Far Horizons, 2015)
'Withered Seeds' in Redemption (WAG, 2017)

Barrakan Tales/Tales of the North:

'Wolf Scout' in Tales of Magic and Destiny (Inklings Press, due 2019)

'Broken Promises' in Another Time Another Place anthology, (Swinburne Students, 2015);

'Full Moon Rises' in Like a Woman anthology, edited by Mirren Hogan, Jeanette O'Hagan and Christina Aitken (Mirren Hogan, 2017)

'Stasia's Stand' in Crossroads, edited Lynn Fowler (Birdcatcher Books, 2017)

Science-Fiction:

'Space Junk' in Mixed Blessings: Genre-lly Speaking, (Breath of Fresh Air Press: 2016)

'Rendezvous at Alexgaia' in Futurevision, edited Delia Strange (1231 Publishing, 2017)

'Project Chameleon' in The Quantum Soul, (Sci-Fi Roundtable, 2017)

'Rookie Mistake' and 'Eating Time' in Mixed Blessings: As Time Goes By, edited by Deb Porter (Breath of Press Air Press, 2017)

'Maroon's Sanctuary' in Gods of Clay, (Sci-Fi Roundtable, 2019)

'Space Triage' in Challenge Accepted (Stephanie Barr, 2019)

Other:

Sandy: Perfect Plans in Let the Sea Roar anthology, By the Light Books, (2015);

To keep up to date with new releases – sign up to my newsletter http://eepurl.com/bbLJKT

Heart of the Mountain: a novella

Twins Delvina and Retza's greatest desire is to be accepted as prentices by their parents' old crew when they stumble across a stranger. Trapped under the mountain, young Zadeki's only thought is to escape home to his kin. Peril awaits all three youngsters. Will they pull apart or work together to save the underground realm?

Heart of the Mountain is the first novella in the Under the Mountain series.

Amazon: https://www.amazon.com/dp/B01J74G9I6/
Elsewhere: https://www.books2read.com/u/4jMrvm

Blood Crystal: a novella

The underground realm is under attack from mad Overseer Uzza and the Crystal Heart is failing. As things become desperate, Twins Delvina and Retza must brave a treacherous journey to seek help from Zadeki and his people. What are the twins prepared to do to save their realm and those they love from certain destruction?

Blood Crystal is the exciting sequel to Heart of the Mountain.

Available on Amazon and other retailers:
http://books2read.com/u/47ZAvL

Akrad's Children

Caught between two cultures, a pawn in a deadly power struggle, Dinnis longs for the day his father will rescue him and his sister from the sorcerer Akrad's clutches. But things don't turn out how Dinnis imagines and his father betrays him. Will he seek revenge for wrongs like his sister or forge a different destiny?

Akrad's Children is the first book in the Akrad's Legacy series

Available on Amazon and other retailers:
http://books2read.com/u/31xWMM

Ruhanna's Flight and other Stories

Ruhanna's Flight and other stories includes previously pubished and brand new stories set in the world of Nardva. A delightful introduction to Jeanette O'Hagan's fantasy world of engaging characters and stirring adventures.

"This author has the gift of immersing a reader in a different world and caring about the people in the world." Amazon Review.

Available on Amazon and other retailers:
http://books2read.com/u/mKKeJE